José Díaz Fernández

Red October in Asturias

edition
Adolfo Campoy-Cubillo

English Translation
Paul Southern

- STOCKCERO -

1st. Stockcero edition: 2021

ISBN: 978-1-949938-09-8
Library of Congress Control Number: 2021947527

Set in Linotype Granjon font family typeface
Printed in the United States of America on acid-free paper.

Published by Stockcero, Inc.
3785 N.W. 82nd Avenue
Doral, FL 33166
USA
stockcero@stockcero.com
www.stockcero.com

José Díaz Fernández

Red October in Asturias

edition
Adolfo Campoy-Cubillo

English Translation
Paul Southern

Contents

Introduction

On October 4, 1934, thousands of Spanish workers went on a strike that has been considered by many as one of the key events that led to the Spanish Civil War. The general strike had been called by the Spanish Socialist Party (PSOE) and its trade union, the General Workers Union (UGT). The strike had also received lukewarm support from the Spanish Communist Party (PCE) and the anarchist trade union (CNT/FAI) which competed with the PSOE for the workers' vote. The strike was motivated by the victory of the conservatives in the 1933 national elections which had made possible the centrist government of Alejandro Lerroux's Radical Republican Party (PRR) with the support of the Confederation of Autonomous Right Parties (CEDA). When the CEDA withdrew its support from the PRR, demanding to bring its own leaders into the government, the left feared that the ascent to power of the Catholic right would endanger the Spanish Second Republic instituted in 1931. This fear was justified by the blatant disregard for democracy that José María Gil Robles, president of the CEDA, had expressed throughout the electoral campaign. In one of the political rallies held that year, Gil Robles had said: "Democracy is not an end for us, but a means to conquer the State. When the time comes, Parliament should submit to our will or we will make it disappear" (Elorza, 203).

However, the success of the strike throughout Spain was uneven. It was strongly supported in Asturias and

Catalonia where the workers were well organized and armed, but only partially successful in areas like Madrid, Andalusia, and Aragón and even less so in the rest of Spain. The memory of the repression of the June 1934 peasant strike and the lack of leaders to help radicalize the strike into an open confrontation with the government contributed to its demise.

The original proposal to form a leftist platform was the initiative of the Workers and Peasants Block (BOC), a small Catalan Marxist party. The proposal gained pace after the 1933 conservative victory in the general elections. The Workers Alliance against Fascism, as the leftist platform was initially known, was opposed by the Catalan Communist Party and the Catalan section of the anarcho-syndicalist CNT. After offering its support to the Workers Alliance, the Socialist Catalan Union (USC) abandoned it to side with the Catalan Republican Party (ERC). This further debilitated the Alliance since the Catalan PSOE and the other parties that supported it had only a limited following in Catalonia. As the Workers Alliance initiative declined in Catalonia, Francisco Largo Caballero, leader of the PSOE, rescued the project of a workers alliance in an attempt to move away from the traditional reformist strategy of his party. The Workers Alliance was successfully organized in some areas of Madrid, Andalusia, and Asturias serving as the platform to promote the 1934 general strike.

The ultimate goal of the general strike was not clearly defined. In the two regions where the general strike gained momentum, the justifications associated to it presented important differences. Lluís Companys, president of the Catalan regional government (Generalitat), proclaimed the Catalan Federated State within what he described as the

Spanish Federal Republic on October 6. Companys was eventually detained by General Domingo Batet and an emergency regional government (the *Consell de la Generalitat*) with members of the traditionalist *Lliga Regionalista de Catalunya* as well as Lerroux's PRR was put in place.

In Asturias, the general strike was not associated to issues of national identity and contested sovereignty. The general strike here focused only on workers' rights and aimed to prevent the erosion of the benefits gained up to that point. Asturias was the region where the general strike was supported by the largest percentage of the workers and where it remained active for the longest time. The Asturian revolt continued days after workers in all other regions had resigned themselves to going back to work.

The general objective of the strike was vaguely defined from its inception. As historian Santos Juliá explains, the PSOE had two separate conceptions of revolution. The first conceived revolution as a reformist process in which the abdication of the king and the declaration of the Republic were seen as tools to bring about a socialist society. The second form of revolution was understood as a violent seizure of power that could be justified in the event that the spirit of the Republic was compromised by the conservative political parties (Juliá, 116-118). For many of the leaders of the PSOE, the October 1934 strike was intended to send a clear message to the CEDA: any attempt to derail the reformist agenda of the Spanish Second Republic would be met with the staunch opposition of the left. The leadership of the PSOE had anticipated an armed confrontation as a result of the general strike and prepared for it. Indalecio Prieto, socialist Minister of public works, ordered a purchase of arms from Portugal that were to arrive in Asturias aboard the steamship Turquesa. The shipment was intercepted by the Spanish Civil Guard, but the miners had already been stockpiling weapons and stealing explosives from the mines. Despite all these preparations, the ultimate goal of the PSOE was, according to historian Adrian Shubert, to secure the success of the general strike (268). Andrés Saborit, secretary general of the PSOE, scolded the workers imprisoned at the Carcel Modelo in Oviedo saying: "Nobody ordered you to start the revolution. The order was for a strike" (qtd. in Solano Palacio, 46).

Unlike the political elites on the left who saw the victory of the conservative forces as a threat to the Republic, the bulk of the working class interpreted it as further proof that the Republic had already failed to deliver on its promises. Many among the rank and file of the PSOE, accordingly, understood the call to a general strike as a literal call to arms to bring about a socialist revolution. It was only in Asturias, however, that the revolutionary drive of the workers coincided with a concerted effort on the part of the regional trade unions, access to weapons, and, most importantly, a rapidly deteriorating economic situation that contributed to the radicalization of the miners.

The decline of the mining industry had increased exponentially with the arrival of the Spanish Second Republic. The Spanish coal market was protected by tariffs from the more competitively priced coal produced in Northern Europe. The large infrastructural works undertaken under the Primo de Rivera dictatorship in the 1920s had helped keep the industry afloat, but as the dictatorship came to an end and the Republic turned its attention to agrarian reform, coal prices plummeted and unemployment among miners grew at a rapid pace.

The revolutionary drive of the miners indicated not only a divide between the political elites and their political base, but also a generational divide among the miners. The Asturian Miners Union (SMA), which was part of the UGT, had traditionally followed the lead of the PSOE for moderate reformist actions. The leadership of the SMA had even complained about the lack of political engagement of the younger generation during the 1920s. Manuel Llaneza, leader, and founder of the SMA, had complained that the younger generation of miners:

> does not know nor want to know our history, does not understand nor want to understand that they have lived in an extremely unusual time, and that instead of dedicating itself to the conquest of knowledge to raise themselves from their condition of inferiority they let themselves be seduced by the glitter of a flame. (*El Socialista* 15 May 1922).

As the economic bonanza of the Primo de Rivera years came to an end, the younger generation that had not known the hardships of state repression in previous strikes, particularly the repression of the 1917 general strike, began demanding that the SMA adopt more aggressive positions. Many of the mining companies like the Mieres plant, the fourth largest producer in the region, went bankrupt. The mine owners demanded higher tariffs from the government and increased productivity with lower wages for the workers. As unemployment increased among workers and those that still had a job saw their acquisitive power rapidly decrease, the divide between the younger, radicalized miners and the older workers that often occupied positions of responsibility in the SMA increased. The miners' union demanded that the mining industry be nationalized and that the Spanish government invested in a viability programme. Ultimately, the SMA was unable to negotiate improvements that could satisfy the needs of their base in part because, as Andrés Saborit indicated, "in his heart of hearts Llaneza [leader of the SMA] felt the owners were right"(qtd. In Shubert, 274). Finding itself in the position of having to lead from the rear, the SMA tried to appease its base by radicalizing its rhetoric. In an article published in *El Socialista* in April 25 of 1934, Teodomiro Menéndez, Socialist deputy for Asturias, said:

> [T]he Socialist Party and the UGT are ready for the struggle. Germany and Italy provide highly tragic lessons. What has cost us so much to achieve, both politically and socially, we will defend with acts of supreme heroism and passion. At the cry of the Republic in danger our political and trade union organizations will throw themselves into a struggle which will have the makings of an epic (qtd. in Shubert 279).

For the rank and file of the SMA, Menéndez's words were an invitation to start a revolutionary uprising, the Socialist deputy for Asturias, however, had hoped that the threat of a revolution would suffice to improve the situation. In the opinion of historian Paul Preston, the revolutionary rhetoric of the Socialist leaders amounted to little more than a bluff, an unsubstantiated threat with which they hoped to satisfy their membership (161-5). Despite attempts by Azaña and other leaders to warn workers of the dangers of resorting to armed confrontation, the threat of an imminent revolution continued to be repeated by Socialist leaders like Largo Caballero and Indalecio Prieto. The rhetorical radicalization of the PSOE, rather than serving to restrain the actions of the conservative government, played directly into the hands of the CEDA that used the revolutionary threat as justification to demand a more active role in the government.

The CEDA staged its assault on the State in a march scheduled for late August in Covadonga, the starting point of the reconquest of Spain. Comparing the Left to the Moorish invaders, Gil Robles incited Spaniards to fight the separatist rebellion in Catalonia and the revolutionary threats of the Socialist infidels "with ecstasy, with paroxysms" (qtd. in Preston 166). Gil Robles' warlike rhetoric was not only a response to the threats of revolution from the Left, but a deliberate attempt to escalate the situation. "Sooner or later," he wrote in his memoirs, "we would have to face a revolutionary coup. It was preferable to face it from a position of power before the enemy was better prepared" (qtd. in Preston 166).

On 26 September, the CEDA withdrew its support from the government presided over by Ricardo Samper arguing that it was unable to manage the situation and demanding a strong government with CEDA participation. Samper resigned on 1 October and, shortly after, on 4 October, the new cabinet was announced confirming the participation of the CEDA. That same day, Teodomiro Menéndez traveled back to Oviedo from Madrid bringing with him the order for the SMA to go on a "general insurrectional strike" (qtd. in Taibo 172).

The Asturian miners took to the streets the next day and quickly took control of many of the towns along the rivers Aller and Nalón. Mieres, the main mining center in the region, became the epicenter of the revolution. The revolutionary committee, formed by two representatives from the PSOE, two from the CNT, two from the PCE, and one from the BLOC proclaimed the Asturian socialist republic. Several of the plants were converted to produce armored cars and equipment to support the rebellion.

The miners then proceeded to march on Oviedo, the capital of Asturias, successfully taking control of part of the city. Throughout the next days, the siege of Oviedo was fought block by block with the miners using dynamite as one of their main weapons. During the confrontations, the Sacred Chamber of the cathedral and the university were badly damaged by the revolutionaries. The destruction of both historical landmarks was presented by the Spanish government as evidence of the brutality of the revolution. The assault and robbery of the Bank of Spain in Oviedo was the other episode that clouded the reputation of the Asturias revolution. The fourteen million pesetas stolen from the bank were never recovered. According to Paco Ignacio Taibo's first edition of his account of the events, part of the money was used to pay the local merchants that had until that point been paid with vouchers issued by the revolutionary committee. A big percentage of the money was used to finance the revolutionary daily *Avance* while the rest of what the revolutionist leaders were able to recuperate was kept in French and Belgian accounts (142).

Diego Hidalgo, Minister of War, called in General Francisco Franco and General Manuel Goded to assist with the repression of the uprising. Historian Paul Preston suggests that the reason why Franco and Goded were called was because López Ochoa, Chief of the General Staff, was a freemason and a personal friend of Manuel Azaña, Prime Minister of the Republic until the PRR gained power in 1933 (168). Judging by the speed with which Franco was able to order the Spanish Legion and Colonial Troops from Morocco to Asturias, it appears that Hidalgo and Franco had agreed on a plan of action before the general strike began. Ironically, the racial imagery invoked by the CEDA during its march in Covadonga was reversed by the deployment of Moroccan soldiers from the Spanish Colonial Army. If the call to regain control of the homeland from the communist infidels had helped raise support for the CEDA, the legendary cruelty of the Colonial Troops spread terror among the civilian population. The Spanish army surrounded the miners with General Bosch and his column advancing to Oviedo from the south, Colonel Yagüe with the Moorish troops and Foreign Legion from the east, and López Ochoa from the west.

By all accounts, the repression of the miners' strike was viciously heavy handed. Franco saw the strike as an existential threat to the conservative order that he had sworn to uphold. He considered the miners' insurrection as a "frontier war, and its fronts are Socialism, Communism, and any other ideology that attacks civilization to replace it with barbarism" (qtd. in Preston *Franco...* 138). Franco understood his mission as being a war of extermination. When one of the officers in charge of the Spanish colonial troops expressed his doubts about whether the troops would be willing to shoot at civilians, Franco ordered that he be replaced with Colonel Yagüe. The same happened with Ricardo de la Fuente Bahamonde, whom Franco suspected of sympathizing with the miners. The bombardment of the Asturian workers' neighborhoods was considered by many officers as an unjustified and brutal action.

According to historian Stanley Payne, the number of casualties for the rebels was close to 1,300 (1,100 of these in

Asturias) while the number of casualties sustained by the army and police was approximately 450 (92). The revolutionaries carried out close to forty summary executions while the army carried out an equal number. The aftermath of the military repression of the insurrection was handled in significantly different ways by the generals in charge of it. López Ochoa negotiated the surrender of the miners with Belarmino Tomás, one of the miners' leaders, thus allowing for an orderly end to the conflict in the areas under his supervision. Colonel Yagüe, on the other hand, allowed his soldiers to carry out the looting and harassment of the civilian population that was a common practice among the colonial troops. Once the strike ended, Hidalgo, probably advised by Franco, tasked Major Lisardo Doval, Civil Guard commander, with the identification and punishment of the revolutionaries which he carried out without mercy. Doval arrested close to 1,500 men, many of whom were tortured while in prison. Teodomiro Menéndez was kept in an isolation cell for over two months in the prison of Oviedo where he was visited by a delegation of the Socialist party after he jumped from one of the open corridors. Efforts to report on the situation of the imprisoned workers were often met with hostility or even violence. Journalist Luís de Sirval was assassinated by Dimitri Ivan Ivanov, an officer of the Spanish Foreign Legion, when he was about to file an article denouncing the circumstances in which Aida Lafuente, a young Asturian girl, had died while fighting against the soldiers in the siege of Oviedo. According to Paco Ignacio Taibo, Aida was probably shot by a firing squad minutes after surrendering to the Spanish Foreign Legion (2013: 415-7). Ivanov was acquitted of first degree murder and charged with involuntary manslaughter. The light sentence and obfuscation of Ivanov's responsibility in Sirval's death was condemned in a manifesto signed by Miguel de Unamuno, Julián Besteiro, Antonio Machado, and other prominent Spanish intellectuals of the time. As the brutality of the repression became known internationally, the government took actions to present itself as neutral and even-handed. Several soldiers and police officers were tried and six senior officers of the Civil Guard were sentenced to prison. In the end, however, both Lisardo Doval and Manuel Hidalgo were forced to resign because the brutality of the repression became a source of international embarrassment for the government.

Although journalistic coverage of the strike was tightly controlled by state censorship, the events of October generated a considerable amount of literature covering different genres including political pamphlets, witness memoirs, and fictionalized accounts. Political pamphlets like Gordon Ordás' "Por la salud del régimen. La represión en las provincias de Asturias, León y Palencia" were published clandestinely in an effort to force the government to follow due process. The government published its own pamphlet "La revolución de Octubre en España: La rebelión del gobierno de la generalidad" to counter the information presented by Ordás and others. Many of the main protagonists of the insurrection also published their own version of the events. Fernando Solano Palacios, one of the leaders of the CNT in Mieres, published *La revolución de octubre: Quince días de comunismo libertario en Asturias*, Diego Hidalgo explained the reasons why he was forced to resign in *¿Por qué fui lanzado del Ministerio de la Guerra?* and López Ochoa presented his analysis of the siege of Oviedo in *Campaña militar de Asturias en octubre de 1934* (1936). The strike was closely followed outside Spain and was portrayed by a young Albert Camus in his play *Révolte dans les Asturies*. The left and the right struggled to impose their interpretation of the events in the arena of public opinion. Liberals and conservatives were well aware that the memorialization of the events had much more political significance than the outcome of the strike itself.

José Díaz Fernández's contribution to the memorialization of the events of 1934 is remarkable for its moderation. Compared to Manuel Benavides' *La revolución fué así* (1935) or even Margarita Nelken's *Por qué hicimos la revolución* (1935) that contributed as much to the rhetorical and ideological radicalization of the left as López Ochoa's and Hidalgo's accounts did for the right, Díaz Fernández's narrative strikes a difficult balance. *Octubre rojo en Asturias* is certainly sympathetic with the miners' demands, but Díaz Fernández's account is carefully structured as an invitation to reflect on the consequences of an ill-advised direct confrontation with Gil Robles' authoritarian government without siding with the conservatives. In an article published in the Diario de Aragón on 7 May, 1936 as the political radicalization in Spain was reaching its climax prior to the 18 July insurrection of General Franco, Díaz Fernández argued that:

> Fascism cannot be fought only with police-like strategies, although we have to say that if the democratic system does not become powerful and feared, it will be devoured by its adversaries in very little time. It is a mistake made by many radical individuals to believe that the revolution should be organized under the protection of the Popular Front. Fascism is what actually begins to manifest itself since in an

> atmosphere of distrust and disorder no one can rule, and the soul of fascism is social disillusionment (2006: 480).

Díaz Fernández was not blind to the limitations of Julián Besteiro's reformist Socialism, but he was well aware that any accomplishment in securing workers' rights was dependent on their institutionalization in the bourgeois order rather than on the overthrowing the social order itself.

Octubre rojo en Asturias can be considered as a documentary novel, a variation of the proletarian novel that gained popularity during the late 1920s and 1930s in Spain. Joaquín Arderius' *Campesinos* (1931), César Arconada's *Los pobres contra los ricos* (1934), and Ramón J. Sender's *Viaje a la aldea del crimen* (1934) had resorted to the same genre before him in order to denounce the injustices of Spanish society at the beginning of the twentieth century.

The interest of proletarian writers in the documentary is not surprising since they had always sought immediacy rather than nuance in their fiction. In the words of César Vallejo, proletarian novelists, and revolutionary art in general should always:

> Be as direct, simple, and raw as possible. An implacable realism. Minimal elaboration. Emotion should be sought after via the shortest path: point-blank. A close-up type of art. Avoid nuance and beating around the bush. Everything should be raw, angles and no curves, but heavy, brutal, as it is in the trenches (qtd. in Fuentes 126).

Like other accounts of the events of 1934, Díaz Fernández structured his narrative around what had come to be understood as the seminal moments of the insurrection: the announcement of the strike, the assassination of Captain Nart, the destruction of the Sacred Chamber and the university, and the surrender of the miners. The diegetic time of *Octubre rojo en Asturias* follows the timeline of events closely without major omissions. It begins with the call for a general strike and concludes as Ramón Tol escapes to France via Portugal, after the third and last revolutionary committee decides to surrender to the army.

If Vallejo demanded a direct and raw style for revolutionary art, conservative depictions of class warfare were equally interested in gruesome narratives that emphasized the evils of the revolution. These conservative narratives often resorted to the traditional schema of the Christian martyr to eulogize the victims of the revolutionaries' violence. Liberal and conservative narratives often fed from each other in an escalation of rhetorical violence; as Bunk explains, "leftist texts also employed familiar religious imagery to celebrate their own fallen heroes (66). The martyrology narrative, for example, was also prominent among liberal representations of the strike that, despite the strong anti-clericalism that characterized them, also emphasized the scenes of torture and agony of the revolutionaries at the hands of the army. Victor Salazar's *El presidiario número 317* and Solano Palacio's *La revolución de octubre* are clear examples of how the left appropriated the martyrology narrative to convey the violence of the repression effectively. Like the pamphlet "Los crimenes de la reaccion espanola," published by the Spanish section of the Comitern Agency International Red Aid (SRI) in 1935, Salazar and Solano highlighted the gory details of the repression in an effort to connect with their readership on an emotional level. Díaz Fernández's description of the events included numerous scenes highlighting the brutality of the revolution and its repression. The depiction of violence in

Octubre rojo en Asturias helped to underscore the unequal encounter between the poorly armed miners and the forces of order. Díaz Fernández, however, deviates from the canon of proletarian fiction in that he avoids making violence the focal point of his story. In the case of *Octubre rojo en Asturias*, depictions of violence have the opposite effect, they promote detachment from the action rather than emotional identification with the events being narrated. As Díaz Fernández explains in his introduction to José Canel's chronicle: "The revolution in Asturias should be judged generously in accordance within a historical criterion, without masking its mistakes or adding to its cruelty." (15). Throughout his narration, Díaz Fernández underscores the senseless toll that the armed confrontation takes on both the miners and the forces of order. The death of Gerardo Monje, shot down shortly after Gerardo had gunned down the lieutenant who was trying to intimidate the miners into surrendering, is one of the many episodes in which Díaz Fernández resorts to violence to help the reader gain critical distance from the events.

Octubre Rojo en Asturias is narrated from the perspective of José Canel, a first-hand witness of the revolution according to Díaz Fernández's introduction. Canel, as Díaz Fernández indirectly admitted in an article published in *El Liberal* in August of 1935, was his fictionalized alter ego, a rhetorical device designed to facilitate the narration of events that he had probably learnt from several witnesses. Canel's voice, however, other than maintaining the diegetic coherence of the story, is practically silent throughout the narrative. We know nothing about Canel's origins and involvement in the revolution. In fact, we do not have an individual protagonist in *Octubre rojo en As-*

turias, but rather a choral protagonist comprising the different miners and soldiers that move the narrative forward collectively. The first individual character in Díaz Fernández's narrative, Gerardo Monje, does not appear until page eight, and then, like "Red Head" or Ampurdián, he dies a few pages later. Their role in the narrative is of relative importance. These individual characters become a focal point of the story only inasmuch as they help exemplify the idealistic abnegation that Díaz Fernández associates with the proletarian collective that they represent.

The collective protagonist of *Octubre rojo en Asturias* evokes the Russian revolutionary films that the *Cineclub Español* sessions organized by Ernesto Giménez Caballero had helped to make popular among Spanish intellectuals. In the presentation of one of these sessions in 1930, Julio Álvarez del Vayo indicated that

> [i]t is the people who become the background to the film's action thus becoming a terrifying chunk of life... In Russian films, the dramatology of the masses does not exclude the presence of great actors, who, on occasion, as in Eisenstein's films, are actors for the first time (qtd. in Román Gubern .335).

As Giménez Caballero's Cineclub Español became inactive shortly before the arrival of the Spanish Second Republic, Ricardo María de Urgoiti and Luís Buñuel launched the Cineclub Proa-Filmófono that would concentrate almost exclusively on Soviet films. Eisenstein's *October: Ten Days That Shook The World* was among the first films shown by Urgoiti and Buñuel in 1932. The list of film societies "associated with non-commercial workerist or cultural groups" increased so rapidly during the following year that movie critic Juan Piqueras proposed the creation of a federation of film societies (2012: 194). Díaz Fernández, like the intellectuals of the Edad de Plata was familiar with the main tenets of Eisenstein's cinema, whose work had been amply commented on in the Spanish press. The characteristics of Eisenstein's work, "its didactic and political intent, its pathos and its intellectual yet popular quality," could easily be applied to *Octubre rojo en Asturias* (Purkey 78) although the same could be said for most of the proletarian novels produced in Spain during the 1920s and 1930s.

Díaz Fernández's chronicle of the Asturian revolution represents an effort to overcome his own aesthetic manifesto, *El Nuevo Romanticismo* (1930), a passionate call for a return to a humanized art, as opposed to the dehumanized avant-garde art that Ortega y Gasset had criticized. New Romanticism was an attempt to combine the discoveries of experimental art and the political commitment of the proletarian novel. In its rejection of the frivolous avant-garde and its embrace of reality in all its political complexity, New Romanticism was informed by the pragmatic engagement with world affairs that the Neue Sachlichkeit had been advocating for in Germany at the same time.

In response to those who accused politically engaged art of being mere propaganda rather than literature, Díaz Fernández responded in *El Nuevo Romanticismo* that:

> Nobody expects the work of art to be political nor to convey a proselitist message in favor of one party or another. This would be alien to art. What we are asking for is to pay attention to those topics that are susceptible to receiving artistic representation and that intrinsically have moral value. (28)

According to Díaz Fernández's aesthetic manifesto, an

engaged, avant-garde literature could contribute to raising political awareness by providing readers with a defamiliarized depiction of conservative ideology that promoted social inequality. The *literatura de avanzada*, as the New Romantics called it, could not help being politically enlightening inasmuch as it helped to deconstruct the unfair social hierarchies that conservatives had helped to naturalize.

By 1934, Díaz Fernández seems to have abandoned his commitment to an engaged avant-garde literature that he had advocated for in *El nuevo romanticismo*. His commitment to social reform had not waned, but his confidence in the enlightening power of the avant-garde had certainly diminished. His straightforward account of the revolution makes few concessions to literary experimentation. In the four years between the publication of *El nuevo romanticismo* and *Octubre rojo en Asturias* many things had changed. The increasing radicalization of Spanish politics and the need to mobilize the masses in response to the certain threat that the CEDA government represented called for a much more explicit form of art. And yet, it would be misguided to dismiss *Octubre rojo en Asturias* as just a political pamphlet. It is a political pamphlet that seeks to use the rhetorical discoveries of the avant-garde to promote a nuanced mobilization of the population. Among the many moments in *Octubre Rojo* that exemplify his use of *literatura de avanzada* is the frantic car drive of two members of the socialist party (nineteen-year-old, Lucero, and his more senior co-driver) as they try to escape a group of imaginary soliders. Unable to drive fast enough to escape his own hysterical fears, the co-pilot ends up killing Lucero

'Faster! Faster, they're coming!'

> 'Nobody's coming, man!'
> 'Faster!'
> 'We're doing eighty; it won't go any faster.'
> But the madman was standing up in the car and no matter how much his comrade tried to calm him down, he could not. He took out a cut-throat razor and gave the driver a terrible slash across the neck, saying,
> 'Take that. You're not going to turn us over to the revolutionaries.' (page number in this edition)

The disturbing image captures the spiral of fear that the revolution has become with one quick scene, very much reminiscent of the revolutionary films Díaz Fernández had drawn from for inspiration. His narrative is certainly informed by the radicalized rhetoric of the time, but his goal, as previously, was not to escalate, but rather, de-escalate the conflict in a final effort to preserve the, by then fatally wounded, Spanish Second Republic.

Adolfo Campoy-Cubillo
2021

Bibliography.

Bunk, Brian D. "'Your Comrades Will Not Forget': Revolutionary Memory and the Breakdown of the Spanish Second Republic, 1934-1936" *History and Memory*. 14 no. 1-2. 65-92

Camus, Albert. *Revolte Dans Les Asturies: Piece En 4 Actes : Essai De Creation Collective*. Alger: E.C, 1936.

Díaz Fernández, José. Octubre Rojo en Asturias. Madrid: Agencia General de Librería y Artes Gráficas, 1935.

__________. "Una política de Frentes Populares" *Prosas*. 479-481. Santander: Fundacion Santander Central Hispano, 2006.

__________. "Si no hubiera mañana. Los contrarrevolucionarios." José Díaz Fernández. *Prosas*. 471-473. Santander: Fundacion Santander Central Hispano, 2006.

__________. *El Nuevo Romanticismo*. Doral: Stockcero, 2013.

Elorza, Antonio. Carmen López Alonso. (1989), *Arcaísmo y modernidad. Pensamiento político en España. Siglos XIX-XX*. Madrid: Historia 16, 1989.

Fuentes, Victor, and de L. M. Tunon. *La Marcha Al Pueblo En Las Letras Espanolas : 1917-1936*. Madrid: Ediciones de la Torre, 2006.

Gubern, Roman. *Proyector De Luna: La Generacion Del 27 Y El Cine*. Barcelona: Anagrama, 1999.

___________. *Luis Bunuel: The Red Years, 1929-1939*. Madison: University of Wisconsin Press, 2012.

Hidalgo, Diego. *Por Que Fui Lanzado Del Ministerio De La Guerra?: Diez Meses De Actuacion Ministerial*. Madrid: Espasa-Calpe, S.A, 1934.

Llaneza, Manuel. *El Socialista* 15 May 1922.

Lopez, de O. P. E. *Campana Militar De Asturias En Octubre De 1934: Narracion Tactico-Episodica*. Madrid: Yunque, 1936.

Payne, Stanley G. *The Collapse of the Spanish Republic, 1933-1936: Origins of the Civil War*. New Haven: Yale University Press, 2006.

Preston, Paul. *The Coming of the Spanish Civil War: Reform, Reaction and Revolution in the Second Republic*. London: Routledge, 1994.

___________. *Franco: Caudillo De Espana*. Barcelona: Debate, 2015.

Purkey, Lynn C. *Spanish Reception of Russian Narratives, 1905-1939: Transcultural Dialogues*. Woodbridge: Tamesis, 2013.

Santos Juliá. "Los socialistas y el escenario de la futura revolución." in Jackson, Gabriel. *Octubre 1934: : Cincuenta Anos Para La Reflexion*. Madrid: Siglo XXI de Espana, 1985.

Shubert, Adrian. "Revolution in Self-defence: the Radicalization of the Asturian Coal Miners, 1921–34." *Social History* 7 no. 3 (2008): 265-282.

Solano Palacio, Fernando. *La revolucion de octubre: Quince dias de comunismo libertario en Asturias*. Barcelona: El Luchador, 1936.

Taibo, Paco I. *Asturias 1934: 2*. Madrid: Ed. Jucar, 1984.
___________. *Asturias 1934*. Barcelona: Planeta, 2013.

Red October in Asturias

Prologue

The first thing of note for whomever dispassionately examines the Spanish October, rather we should say the Asturian October, as only in Asturias did a true armed uprising take place, is the lack of a supportive environment. Spanish society was not prepared for the inherent watchwords of the social revolution and the dictatorship of the proletariat.[1] It lacked a favorable social climate; bourgeois defenses were not spent, neither was the State in decay. It was an enormous error by the socialists, who moved without transition from governmental collaborationism to class revolution.

Although many of the things I am going to say in this prologue are in the collective memory, I have little alternative but to repeat them. When on reflection the reader makes a comparison with the events of October, he will view them with greater clarity, given that historical events do not happen by spontaneous generation; they are always the consequence of previous events.

The first thing to recall of the political antecedents of

---

1 Díaz-Fernández's comments foreshadow Salvador Madariaga's argument in *España: ensayo de historia contemporánea* that the radicalization of the Socialist party, as well as the radicalization of the right, contributed to the downfall of the Spanish Second Republic. According to Madariaga's insightful reading, however, the problem of the Spanish Second Republic was not that the bourgeois State was not in decay, but rather that Spain had not managed to transition to a modern State. Although the Spanish Second Republic presented itself as a Republic of intellectuals, Madariaga was quite dismissive of the ability of Spanish intelligentsia to lead the country. In his response to Madariaga's book, Antonio Gramsci agreed that the role of Spanish intellectuals in the Spanish revolution was a highly idiosyncratic one.

the uprising is how they survived the change of regime. This was not the fruit of a triumphal revolution. Yes, there was the pressure of public opinion against the monarchy because the king above all, was blamed for the military dictatorship of Primo de Rivera. The conservative and neutral masses, who had initially sympathized with the dictatorship, due to antipathy with the same old political class, were alienated by the monarchy which, despite that extreme measure, was unable to resolve any of the national problems. Consequently, when after seven years of forced electoral abstention, the nation was consulted, it chose republican candidates.[2] One of the king's ministers noted the event in the following way, 'It's a country which went to bed a monarchy and awoke a republic.' My readers know that the provisional government, comprising three socialists, had prepared for the king's flight, and that King Alfonso[3] left Cartagena as a monarch who was withdrawing rather than abdicating. He apparently said, 'I

2 Díaz Fernández is referring here to the proclamation of the Spanish Second Republic after the Primo de Rivera dictatorship. The initial popularity enjoyed by the dictator, who was seen as a viable alternative to years of incompetent politicians, quickly dissipated at the end of the 1920s. The reasons that explain the demise of the Primo de Rivera dictatorship are complex and interrelated. The main one is the economic downturn that put an end to the infrastructure projects that the dictator had been undertaking during the first half of his regime. As James H. Rial explains, although unemployment figures did not begin to be collected until the end of the dictatorship and the data available only show modest increases in unemployment, it is more than likely that a considerable portion of the working population had entirely withdrawn from the workforce by 1930 which would explain why they did not show up in the statistics (229). Primo de Rivera lost the support of Catalan and Basque nationalists who were expecting him to decentralize the government. Industrialists and small business owners resented the active role that the UGT, the socialist union which had agreed to collaborate with the dictator, had attained under the regime.

3 The departure of Alfonso XIII surprised the conservative segments of Spanish society that had counted on him as a guarantor of the traditional order. The *Carlistas* pledged to bring down the Spanish Second Republic by force while others like the Catholic Church, attempted to co-opt the reformist attempts of the new government.

follow tradition.' It was the tradition of his grandmother and his great-grandmother who driven by their mistakes, also migrated to Paris; but without abdicating. It is known that left-wing politicians predominated in the government, nonetheless the most moderate men, Alcalá Zamora, Lerroux and Maura[4], were those who gave a conservative tone to the nascent republic.

To what is owed this preponderance of moderate forces which had to sustain themselves throughout the different Republican governments? It was without doubt, the peaceful origin of the Republic. The conservative classes which had distanced themselves from the monarchy looked favorably on the fact that at the head of the new regime was a wealthy, Andalusian landowner, and fiery parliamentarian, who at the time represented the counterrevolution. In Spain Bolshevism was greatly feared during that period. Besides, republicans known as 'the historic ones,' were discredited. They were to be found in monarchical politics in 'opposition to his majesty' and were publicly accused of meekly cohabiting with monarchist

4 Niceto Alcalá Zamora, president of the Second Spanish Republic between 1931 and 1936, and Miguel Maura, Minister of the Interior, were the founders of the Liberal Republican Right party, a group of moderate, Catholic, monarchists converted to Republicanism. Alcalá Zamora and Maura opposed the legislation that aimed to complete the separation of Church and State in Spain. They also complained vehemently against the anti-clerical riots that resulted in the burning of churches and monasteries after the proclamation of the Republic. Alejandro Lerroux gained popularity among the working classes for his campaigns against the governments of the Restoration. When the Primo de Rivera dictatorship came to power, the left wing of his party left to form the Radical Socialist Republican Party of which Díaz Fernández was also a member. Lerroux was the most visible figure of the emerging mass politics, the beginnings of which historian José Álvarez Junco, dates back to the end of the nineteenth century (vii). Lerroux's populist demagoguery gained him the nickname of the Emperor of the Paralelo (Barcelona's Theater district). Lerroux was elected president of the new conservative government that came to power in the 1933 elections.

politicians, without any great concern for the triumph of the Republic.

How did the socialists and left-wing republicans accommodate this conservative influence? They had little faith in the revolutionary capacity of the masses. Socialists, from Pablo Iglesias[5] down, responded to the tactic of reformist socialism. Largo Caballero,[6] later the leader of the revolution, had during the military dictatorship, even belonged, by order of the party, to a senior agency of the monarchical State, representing trade union power. And they were the first to be convinced of the inefficiency of the old republicanism, preferring the converts Alcalá Zamora and Maura, believing them to be more trustworthy. The truth is that they were constantly making protestations of their love for the proletariat, and of the need for major social reforms. The left-wing republicans,

---

5 Pablo Iglesias founded the Spanish Socialist Party (PSOE) in 1879 and *El Socialista* the magazine that became the main tool of communication for the new organization. Díaz Fernández's denunciation of the passive reformism that characterized the early years of the PSOE provides an insightful diagnosis of the limitations that would eventually become characteristic of its interactions with the Primo de Rivera dictatorship and of its role in the Second Spanish Republic. As Paul Kennedy explains, "[t]he PSOE's rhetorical radicalism belied the party's patent unsuitability for revolutionary activity" (23).

6 Francisco Largo Caballero was one of the leaders of the Spanish Socialist Party (PSOE) and its trade union, the General Workers Union (UGT). He became the head of the party and its trade union in 1925 after the death of its founder Pablo Iglesias. Against the advice of Julián Besteiro, Secretary General of the PSOE, who believed that Spain should undergo a bourgeois revolution before socialists accepted positions in the Spanish government, Largo-Caballero went on to become the Minister of Labor Relations in the first governments of the Second Spanish Republic between 1931 and 1933. Unlike Besteiro, Largo-Caballero believed that collaboration with the bourgeois republican governments would help him defend the interests of the proletariat. As Paul Preston explains, the schism within the PSOE between the followers of Besteiro and Largo-Caballero was not clear cut, "the ideological differences between them were difficult to ascertain since both of them were reformists" (1977: 106) grounded on ideological differences but on the different strategies favored by each leader.

for their part, were new to the political struggle. In a congested democracy, they represented large sectors of opinion which were scarcely articulated in hastily organized, disparate parties, and ended up dividing and atomizing them.

The principal concern of the new leadership, before it convened the *Cortes Constituyentes*, should have been to resolutely confront the country's problems. Instead, it was to establish its new legitimacy, before having provided sustainable solutions for keeping to a minimum the disruption to the life of the State.

The *Cortes Constituyentes* strove to ensure it should not happen, but in the end, they were defeated, not without, in truth, falling victim to serious weaknesses. The elections for the *Cortes Constituyentes* gave a large majority to the socialists and left-wing republicans. The country made efforts to break with the traditional cortex and transform itself by means of new institutions. But from the beginning, one saw the large historical oligarchs survive the dethronement of King Alfonso. The State's secular program unleashed an offensive by the Church. The agrarian reform, brought in to socialize the large farms through the corresponding indemnification of their owners, was trimmed in such a way that it became inefficient and incapable of satisfying the yearning for land by thousands of unemployed farmhands, instead, it aroused the hostility of the landowners.[7] They created a Constitution that looked

---

7 The agrarian reform was one of the most important promises made by the Second Spanish Republic. Shortly after its inauguration, the Spanish Republic began to work on a bill to promote the distribution of land among landless peasants after paying an indemnification to their original owners. The bill was perceived as a threat to the interests of many Spanish aristocrats who held most of the underutilized land and who conspired with General Sanjurjo to organize a *coup d'état* on August 10, 1932. Alejandro Lerroux's connivance with General Sanjurjo was

progressive on paper alone, as the reforms lacked realism owing to the Republican-Socialist government's lack of courage. Azaña and the Justice Minister, Albornoz, were the only ones who dared to undertake reforms of the army, the magistracy, and the church. The Jesuits were dissolved, but they stayed on, housed in Catholic residencies.[8] It was a requirement that education should be the exclusive mission of the State, but colleges belonging to the religious orders continued functioning by means of figureheads. In the end, they created, according to Lassalle's words, a paper Constitution.[9] Actually, it was not the first. The 1812 Constitution of Cadiz,[10] fruit of the liberalism of the day, failed

---

denounced in the pages of *El Socialista*, but never proven. Historian Nigel Townson argues that the conspiracy to topple the Second Spanish Republic must have been financed by Spanish tycoon Juan March (Townson 42). The agrarian reform law was approved shortly after the *coup d'état* failed, but its application proved to be slow and deficient. The underfunded and understaffed Agrarian Reform Institute (IRA) suffered boycotting by the private banking system. The agrarian reform law was promptly revoked when General Franco came to power after the Spanish Civil War.

8 The Society of Jesus, as the Jesuit order is known, had been expelled from Portugal in 1910, it was expelled from Mexico in 1917, and from Spain in 1932 with the arrival of the Spanish II Republic. Jesuits had considerable power in Spanish politics. A relevant example of this in the years that preceded the 1934 Asturias revolution was the efforts of the Asociación Católica Nacional de Propagandistas (ACNP) to co-opt the reformist attempts of the Socialists. Created in 1909, it consisted of prominent conservatives in the press, the judiciary, and liberal professions, this Jesuit influenced organization helped the Confederación Nacional Católico Agraria (CNCA) to gather support against any threats to the Spanish II Republic. According to Paul Preston, the ACNP and the CNCA were so successful "that they shattered completely the hopes that the Socialists had placed in the Republic" (1994, 39)

9 Ferdinand Lassalle in his speech "On the Essence of Constitutions" delivered in 1862, criticized the belief that constitutions automatically granted citizens' rights by saying so in writing. according to him, "Constitutional questions are first and foremost not questions of right but of force; the actual constitution of a nation lies in the real, actual relation of forces existing there, written constitutions are valid and stable only when they correctly express the actual relation of forces in a society" (n.p.)

10 The Political Constitution of the Spanish Monarchy, as the 1812 Constitution of Cadiz was formally known, marks the birth of Hispanic liberalism actively advocating for a limited constitutional monarchy.

to fulfill its promise, thanks to the absolutism of the Bourbons, the inefficacy of the liberals, and the ignorance and compliance of the people. In the *Cortes Constituyentes*, Alcalá Zamora declared himself in disagreement with the Constitution. Despite that, the Republican-Socialist majority elected him President of the Republic - I did not. I was a deputy and not only did I not vote for him, rather I proposed another candidate, despite the outrage of some leftist leaders.

The defeat suffered by the monarchists in the uprising of August 1932, made them think that the Republican regime was stronger than they had originally believed and that it was necessary to use another tactic against it. In order to do that, they financed the anti-Marxist campaign, which although it appeared to be aimed at socialists, also tried to nullify the left-wing Republicans. In the end Alcalá Zamora handed power to Lerroux, who for several days led a Republican Government in appearance, giving way to a hybrid situation which accepted the dissolution of the *Cortes* and the calling of new elections. This took place in November 1933, scarcely two and a half years after the proclamation of the Republic.[11]

In these elections, the 'historic' republicans had already definitively united with the monarchists to end the in-

---

The 1812 Constitution promoted popular political representation through a three-tiered electoral system of deputies, regional governments or *Diputaciones Provinciales*, and local governments for communities of more than one thousand people. Most importantly, the 1812 Constitution secured equal taxation for peninsular and Spanish-American citizens. In limiting the power of the Spanish king, the 1812 Constitution actively triggered the calls for independence of many of the Spanish colonies in America. The 1812 Constitution never came into effect as the Ferdinand VIII abolished it on returning to Spain after the defeat of Napoleon.

11 Díaz Fernández is referring to the triumph of the conservative forces in the 1933 Spanish national elections.

fluence of the democratic elements. They invested large sums of money which the leftists lacked. To make the left's situation worse, the parties that until then had governed jointly began to separate and fragment, distracted by byzantine disputes, while the conservatives united in a solid block. It was then when the socialists, who had just abandoned power, abruptly changed tactics to distance themselves from the leftist republicans. All the traditional forces were then united, while those who had drawn up the Constitution, struggling to give it a moderate tone, were fighting in disarray, faced with an electoral law designed to favor coalition parties, they splintered, lacking conviction and the means of propaganda. There is no doubt the monarchists who appeared in the new *Cortes*, had triumphed – incorporating a majority which, leaving momentarily to one side the problem of the form of Government, it proposed to end all the reforms brought about by the republican-socialist majority in the *Asamblea Constituyente*.

So began concessions to the victorious forces to the point where the concrete process of allowing into Power elements which, like those of Gil Robles, had a monarchical make-up. This party had roundly refused to declare for the republic; its members originated from the Primo de Rivera dictatorship. The moment arrived when Alcalá Zamora accepted a government in which these forces figured. The leftists saw themselves expelled from the party they had created. They realized that legal roads were already blocked, and the revolution alone could save them; but they suffered that uniquely democratic indecision which in other countries gave way to fascism. There was without doubt, a man, Azaña,[12] who proclaimed the need for a national revolution to re-establish the Constitution and the original direction of the regime. But the socialists, their allies of yesterday, had already embarked on an adventure in social revolution after the Russian fashion, without considering that in truth, they lacked a Lenin.

I have already said that socialism in Spain had a reformist tradition. Its most prominent personalities had been ministers in the Republican Government, honestly collaborating in moderate policies. To the extent, that in the religious question they held more conservative views than some leftist republican ministers, for example Albornoz. He once sought to nationalize the railroad industry but met with opposition from the socialists. Clearly, the anti-Marxism of the traditional forces made no sense whatsoever because the socialists had not practised Marxism since coming to power. The anti-Marxism of the right was merely a pretext to draw the Republic into its orbit. On leaving Power the socialists considered themselves as lost to the regime and except for Besteiro, adopted a revolutionary stance. The mutation could not have been more abrupt. The socialists had energetically repressed the communists' and anarchists' impatient demands. With an interval of just a few months, the socialists, not only thoroughly changed their usual tactics, but proclaimed the

12 Manuel Azaña was a Spanish politician and one of the signatories of the Pact of San Sebastian (1924) which united all republican and regionalist parties against the Primo de Rivera dictatorship and the Spanish king, Alfonso XIII. In 1926, Azaña founded with José Giral the Spanish Republican party *Acción Republicana* that would become the leading party in the first government of the Spanish Second Republic. Azaña served first as Minister of War and then as Prime Minister leading some of the most controversial initiatives undertaken by the Spanish Second Republic: the reduction of the Spanish military; the secularization of the Spanish educational system; and an agrarian reform that aimed to distribute land ownership among peasants.

need for a social revolution and tried to concoct the Confederated Proletarian Front. In such circumstances, this Confederated Front was pure utopia. The Spanish proletariat, above all in the regions of the northwest, center and south, are fundamentally anarchist and loyal to the National Confederation of Labor. Due to its ingrained individualism, anarchism has a great tradition in Spain. They do not, therefore, control all the socialist workers' organizations, rather in Catalonia, Levant, Galicia and Andalusia, the mass of the proletariat has an anarcho-unionist hue. The communists also possess important nuclei throughout the Peninsula.

The Socialist Revolution

Proletarian internal struggles are not merely disagreements, but true historic struggles. Consequently, when the socialists called for the social revolution, they were not believed by the rest of the workers' groups. At the last moment, only the communists decided very conditionally to collaborate with them. In order to substitute the Soviet Russian model, the socialists created Workers' Alliances, where apart from the socialist forces; they contained only loose Trotskyite groups and other communist factions which in reality, lacked the support of the masses. The *Confederación General del Trabajo* refused to join the Alliances in all the regions apart from Asturias, where, thanks to the revolutionary drive of the masses, they established the Confederated Front. This goes some way to explain the drive that the armed insurrection had there. The revolutionary organs in many parts lacked sufficient strength. The workers who formed them were educated in the school of socialist reform and were without revolutionary training and experience. Months before they had mobilized in defense of the bourgeois old guard and scarcely without transition, were invited to destroy it. This meant that the revolution would have the character of something improvised which from the outset constituted its failure.

Nor was this the worst of it. The worst was that from the start, the uprising was decentralized. Actually, each region acted alone without responding to an elemental unity of action. While the strictures of the social revolution held, it alienated the fellow feeling and support of the leftist bourgeoisie, it attempted to take advantage of the violent protests in the autonomous regions such as Catalonia and the Basque Country. In Catalonia, there had been no prior revolutionary agreement between the socialists and the Government of the *Generalitat*; but the socialists waited for the rebellion to prevail there by indirect means. It was a complete disaster. The Workers' Alliance lacked weapons and strength. Those who had weapons, failed to use them, or used them incompetently. The army was ordered to put an end in a few hours, to something that was pure fiction. Meanwhile, the influential industrial workers in Catalonia not only ignored the movement but did not even call a peaceful strike.

In the Basque Country, events were different, but the result identical. Socialists and communists, who heralded the social revolution and the dictatorship of the proletariat, allied themselves with the nationalists who represented the most uncompromising bourgeoisie. They were united solely by hatred for a policy which threatened regional freedoms. A governor was all it took to quell the uprising. The truth is that nationalist elements, noting the character of the revolution in the rest of Spain, lay down their weapons. Hundreds of socialist and communist workers heroically died in desperate struggles in Madrid and in other places. In Madrid, the revolution was the isolated action of youthful fighters who fired at the *guardias* from the rooftops. It is not known why, but the proletarian militias failed to act. Only some groups of young activists imbued with a futile, primitive courage, and armed with pistols, fought against the army at the Puerta del Sol, where without leaders or direction, they valiantly perished for an abstract revolutionary ideal.

Asturias has been a different case. The Asturian workers still fought on, ten days after the uprising was extinguished in the rest of Spain. Apart from the forces that held out against the siege of Oviedo, it needed two army corps to attack them from different directions. In order to enter Oviedo, they had to deploy Moroccan colonial troops who formed the vanguard and treated the capital like a city at war. I have already said it was only there where a revolutionary workers front was created. This, combined with the ruggedness of its terrain, led to the emergence of a true revolution, if in truth, deficiently organized. It lacked a military command; instead of being entrusted to experts, it was led by militant socialists of recognized honesty and fighting spirit, but who were absolutely ignorant of the techniques of warfare. For example, the revolutionaries had artillery, but did not know how to deploy it, and the shells failed to explode even when they tried to charge them with dynamite. They neglected the aviation problem which destroyed them and created dejection among the ranks of the workers; they even lacked means of mutual communication. They had no idea about how to select strategic positions.

The Asturian workers showed an extraordinary fighting capability. Why were they the only ones in the whole of Spain who fought with any cohesion and with true revolutionary courage? This is a very interesting theme of proletarian psychology. The Asturian miner is a worker who, combining the traits of the industrial worker, also possesses the primitive drive of the mountain dweller. In the Workers' Clubs, he is in contact with revolutionary ideals which stem from the class struggle, but he is certainly not the urban worker enjoying several of the advantages of civilization; he lives in mountain villages, on the fringes of the coalfields, where he retains the ferocity of the mountain dweller in tandem with a hatred of the powerful. He ignores danger because he lives in the depths of the earth, exposed to firedamp and the daily manhandling of the devastating power of dynamite. Many of these revolutionaries did not fight with such light weapons as rifles or pistols. They fought with cartridges of dynamite. In Oviedo, they could be seen with two or three dynamite cartridge belts around their waists, lighting the cartridges from the cigarettes they were smoking. This, together with a firm trade union discipline, acquired in the old Unions, made for a rebellion of unique importance. For these proletarians, (many of them inclined to Communism, which in recent times had gained great preponderance there) socialist reform had never made inroads, even though outwardly there were great trade union advantages – six-hour days; worker retirement; educational and charitable institutions.[13] It is also true that Asturian mine owners have never understood how to gain their men's respect or introduced technical innovations in the workplace.

However, also in Asturias where they had set up the Confederated Front, a slump in the enthusiasm for anarcho-syndicalism was apparent. In Gijón, where this tendency dominated, the movement lacked the importance it had in the openly socialist areas of Oviedo and in the coalfields. The plan was to take over the capital and proclaim there the dictatorship of the proletariat. Thousands of miners fell on Oviedo and took over the weapons factory. The lack of military leadership meant they were unable to defeat a garrison of barely 2,000 men sheltering in their quarters. Besides, dissensions were soon accentuated by the different tendencies among the members on the revolutionary committees. There were three revolutionary committees in ten days, each one of a different hue.

There is no certainty that the revolutionaries destroyed the city or that the atrocities reported by some newspapers were perpetrated by the miners; an isolated case does not lend any such weight. Several buildings were set alight by aerial bombardment and a theater held by the miners was destroyed by government troops; the miners were generally humane and kindly and respected prisoners, many of them class enemies. What happened in Turón proves the ex-

---

13 According to Adrian Shubert's monograph on the 1934 revolution, the economic boom helped the Socialist mine workers' union (SMA) become one of the strongest in Spain. The union was able to secure better conditions like the seven-hour day, but once markets returned to normal after World War I, the less competitive Spanish mining industry saw a severe reduction in its benefits. Paradoxically, the arrival of the Spanish Second Republic coincided with a deterioration of the working conditions for the miners which led them, particularly the younger ones, to adopt increasingly radical positions (Shubert, 1987)

ception, not the rule. On the other hand, that cannot be said of the repression. After their defeat and surrender, the miners have been treated like men beyond the rule of law. Lastly, the truth is that the fourteen million pesetas 'expropriated' by the Banco de España in Oviedo have been lost. The vans carrying the money were looted by villagers and by the guards themselves. The revolution has failed because it lacked the right social conditions. If the socialists had attempted a movement in defense of the Constitution and the Republic, they would have triumphed. Immediately after their participation in bourgeois governments, it became impossible to improvise the revolutionary spirit for the all-out struggle they wished to create.

The Looters Of The Revolution

This account is written in the manuscript of a witness to the revolution. It says no more than the author of the document has seen with his own eyes. Consequently, he has omitted some of the resounding episodes, as he definitely did not wish to recount anything from memory. It is preferable to ignore an event rather than falsify it.

The narration leads up to the point and the hour when the revolutionaries leave Oviedo. Other no less impressive chroniclers will, without any doubt speak about what happened later. The revolution in Asturias should be judged generously in accordance with a historical criterion, without masking its mistakes or adding to its cruelty. Like so many others, I have felt the anguish of watching blood flow through that country of mine, its struggles and triumphs are imprinted on my heart The devastated streets of Oviedo, her countless ruins, her stricken trees, and her collapsed towers weigh on my soul, because what is more, all this goes hand in hand with my childhood memories. But it pains me just as much as the injustice which made the revolution possible; the heroism of those miners moves me, without any thought of support, they throw themselves into the struggle for an ideal which has ceased to be utopian, and whether well or badly led, offer up their lives to the revolution, because it is all they have.

However, they are faced with their slanderers, the same ones who in October were trembling with panic while disguised and in hiding, only to reappear threatening vengeful accusations. This unworthy bourgeoisie which calls for the death penalty on which they base a political program, can awake nothing else in the working classes other than hatred and repulsion. We have seen certain men and certain parties take advantage of the October Revolution to take over town and provincial councils and agencies that the popular vote had denied them in their day, and replace them with the same old, filthy, and discredited local tyrants. These are the real looters of the revolution. The looters have reached such extremes, that the actual authorities in Oviedo have had to oppose the perpetration of certain acts of vengeance and the completion of certain business deals. They would like to speculate with monies given by the State for the reconstruction of Asturias and put a price on pain while making capital out of the ruins of the wasted city. From here, facing the Spain of tomorrow, I heap contempt on those looters of the revolution.

J. Díaz Fernández

Mieres Starts the Revolution

The First Group -The Miners Advance -The March on Oviedo -The Enlistment- The Battle Fronts.

Mieres was the home of the revolution.[14] It is a large, dark town, spread over a mountain side where a red glow from the metallurgical factories broadcasts its presence. The huge mining valley spreads out from the foothills of Pajares to the gates of Oviedo; it leads to Mieres, where the most important industries, the companies and the technicians' offices are located, and it is where the workers' red painted homes are. In the evening, it swarms with men dressed in coveralls, tired, tousle-haired women with swollen eyes reddened by the heat of the workshops and by the slag heaps, and with dirty, ragged, truculent, little children who go out in search of coal on the riverbanks close to the sluicing places.

At sunset on day five, delegates from the revolutionary committees went out onto all the mountain roads, announcing a general strike and an armed uprising for the following day. The groups from Mieres had no weapons. Nevertheless, they had to get them and so they joined a group of communists and socialists who left at dawn

14 The Mieres plant, the fourth largest producer in the province, went bankrupt in February of 1934. A commission comprised of representatives of the courts, the Sindicato de Minas Asturianas, creditors, shareholders and industrialists took over. The commission was unable to pay the back wages owed to the workers. According to Adrian Shubert, most mining companies were two or three months behind (Shubert 1982, 272).

armed with pistols and shotguns. Without doubt, it was that group which started the revolution. They first went to the small barracks of the *guardia municipal*. It was an easy task there. The reserve *guardias* were asleep on their cots and barely had time to recover from their surprise on seeing some familiar faces among that group. The revolutionaries took their weapons and ammunition and left for a nearby gunsmith's store, where they rapped furiously on the door. The owner peered out of a window and was invited to hand over his weapons.

The storekeeper did not offer any resistance. But before letting the revolutionaries in, he telephoned the barracks of the *Guardia de Asalto*. Consequently, as they began to collect the store's shot guns and cartridges, the *Guardia de Asalto* turned up in a van. The revolutionaries fired before they could get out. Three *guardias* were wounded. The others, believing that their attackers were in larger numbers, retreated to the barracks of the *guardia urbana* where they barricaded themselves in.

But this was the signal for battle. Miners began to arrive from their villages with carbines and pistols. An immense crowd gathered in the Plaza de la Constitución, from where columns of volunteers set out to take the barracks. Several miners went armed with dynamite cartridges, ready to detonate them in case of resistance. And what happened in Mieres, happened almost simultaneously in the other coalfield towns, in Aller, in Pola de Lena and in Turón. By eight-thirty in the morning, all government units in that area had surrendered, but not before putting up some stiff resistance to the revolutionaries. Nevertheless, the avalanche was such that the whole valley was up in arms, like a flooding river carrying all with it.

There were amazing scenes in the Plaza de Mieres. After the surrender of the *Guardia de Asalto*, the masses asked that two who were known for their harsh repression of demonstrations, be handed over to them. The Committee refused. These two *guardias* were wounded and needed to be taken to the emergency hospital. When the crowd witnessed their arrival in the square, protected by workers, some ten men with shotguns came forward demanding to finish them off. The workers were forced to shield them with their own bodies to prevent them from being shot. But in a fit of panic, one of the *guardias* wearing a torn and bloodied uniform, tried to break through the protective cordon. No sooner had he done so than he was killed by two shotgun blasts.

Halfway through the morning, thousands of workers crowded around the Casa del Pueblo, from where the movement's orders were transmitted. The Transport Committee had impounded trucks and cars. The Provisions Committee had centralized the foodstuffs, announcing the abolition of money, instead providing food coupons for the civil population.

Trucks and cars were gathering in front of the Casa del Pueblo, their engines vibrating like impatient beasts. From time to time, in the midst of that tragic hubbub, excited, spirited voices were heard.

'Revolutionary volunteers for Oviedo!

Revolutionary volunteers for Campomanes!'

Men rushed the vans keen to be the first to leave. The majority climbed in without weapons, as there were not enough to go around. The miners were convinced that the decision to enter the fray and face the utmost danger showed that the struggle was more than necessary, inevitable. They almost cheerfully took leave of their friends, and during those awful days it was not unusual to hear chatter and banter coming from the top of the trucks

'Hey buddy, you can also die in the mine, !' shouted one of them, armed with an almost useless, old rifle.

'True, true. I threw my tools into the river yesterday. Long Live the Revolution!'

While they were organizing the fighting expeditions, groups of workers were attacking the gunpowder store and taking charge of the dynamite used in mining work. Others occupied the metallurgic workshops and factories where they formed teams to prepare the bombs which they were to use in the attack. Some of the artefacts were true infernal machines. They contained two packets of dynamite – some forty-two cartridges – and ten kilos of shrapnel made from steel rod trimmings. Many men toiled day and night in these workshops where they manufactured more than five thousand bombs.

The *guardia* barracks which took the longest time to surrender was at Campomanes, a mining town on the Northern Line, bordering León. It was there that a *Guardia Civil* corporal and a few men held out. On hearing the news in Mieres, many revolutionist groups set out; by three o'clock in the afternoon they had managed to overcome the *Guardia Civil* after killing the corporal and gravely wounding two guards. The barracks had contacted León for reinforcements and shortly after, a *Guardia de Asalto* truck appeared with a machine gun readied for action.

By then, the large grouping of miners was master of the town. The *Guardia de Asalto* were undoubtedly unaware that a veritable army awaited them. Scarcely had the truck appeared in one of the streets of Campomanes, before volley fire destroyed half of its personnel. The *guardias* did not even have time to use their machine gun. The survivors threw themselves onto the ground and fanning out, made for the cover of a factory, where within the space of twenty minutes they were annihilated. A corporal and two men alone were able to flee up the hill across country towards León.

The terrain favored the revolutionaries' plans. The entire zone, running from Pajares is a succession of peaks and hills with deep ravines flanked by woodlands, where thousands of men could hide without being seen. The day after the first clash, the miners spontaneously set up a battle front. The committees' orders were labored and indecisive, but the men instinctively understood the demands of war and prepared for the assault. They assumed that forces tasked to defeat them would come from the León Line. Even though enthusiasm had generated the most optimistic rumors announcing the triumph of the proletariat everywhere, the miners were awaiting battle.

In fact, the first military forces, a Palencia cyclist battalion, appeared a few hours later, followed by another two infantry units. It was a very hard fight. The vanguard troops were almost totally overwhelmed, but the remainder, while suffering heavy losses, gained the Vega de Rey position, from where they held out under the miners' constant siege for a week, from 8 October to 16 October, the date when the revolutionary pressure finally slackened.

The march on Oviedo was much easier. Hundreds of miners enlisted for the front. The first battle between government forces and the insurrectionists took place right on the road, at a place known as *Cuesta de la Manzaneda*. The *guardias* occupied the houses from where they intended to block the advancing groups but it was in vain. During continuous heavy fire the revolutionaries occupied the highest hill overlooking the enemy position. The latter had no option other than to abandon it and stage a fighting withdrawal towards the nearby hills. There the *guardias* were hunted down one by one, and after stripping them of their webbing and weapons, the miners marched like a whirlwind on Oviedo, where new and tragic days began.

On the roadway, fate had jumbled up the bodies of *guardias* and of revolutionaries. Next day, farmhands from nearby villages dug a ditch in the side of the hill and buried them in piles, under the droning roar of the first airplanes.[15]

15 The French built the Breguet 19 which was in service with Escuadra No 1 during the Asturian Revolution. This was a two-seater biplane with rear mounted 7.7 mm Vickers machine gun. It could carry up to 472 kilograms bombs located under its fuselage, or 50 kg in vertical bomb bay.

II – THE STRUGGLE IN CAMPOMANES

'THE ARGENTINIAN' AND HIS GROUP - CHAMPAGNE FOR THE PARIAHS - CONFUSION AT THE FRONT-THE ASSAULT - A MYSTERIOUS DEATH.

Around three thousand miners assembled on the Campomanes battle front. Weapons were scarce; there was not enough weaponry until the La Vega Factory in Oviedo fell to the revolutionaries. On the other hand, the miners lacked a stable organization, and as they were operating on their own initiative, their actions were confused. The most basic support services barely functioned. Many young miners had taken sweethearts and wives along with them, and this was the support they relied on. These brave, defiant women encouraged and helped them, but they were an extraordinary obstacle in the fight against the troops.

The first fairly organized groups to arrive came from Moreda. At the head of one of them was a revolutionist who had been outstanding in his determination and courage in the taking of the barracks. His name was Gerardo Monje[16] and he worked as a clerk on various municipal projects. Monje had lived in Buenos Aires and still spoke with an Argentine accent. He was a magnificent shot. He had a *Guardia Civil*'s Mauser and webbing, and his comrades obeyed him as their unquestionable leader. The first thing he did was to name a young coalface

16 Gerardo Monje, like some of the other characters presented by José Díaz Fernández in his fictionalized documentary of the Asturias revolution, may have been a composite of different individuals that participated in the revolt.

worker, Antonio Martín, as his lieutenant. The Campomanes committee charged Monje with the capture of the railroad station at Linares, where according to secret information, there was a food convoy. In contrast, the workers in the town were short of food. They assumed that the station would be defended by military forces and ordered the revolutionaries there to attack it.

Monje deployed his men for battle. But as he reached the vicinity of the station he found only the station master and some railroad workers.

'Well, how stupid!' exclaimed Monje bursting into the station with his men, 'Food is close at hand, yet people are going hungry'

He immediately began to requisition the freight cars. There was flour, vegetables, canned food and even crates of champagne.

Locals who had arrived behind the miners, were keen to join in the looting, wildly pouncing on the food supplies. The 'Argentinian' stopped them. He fired at the feet of the first looters and they stepped back in terror. One, who was more determined and had refused to take any notice, was shot in his right arm. He then said in his thick Argentinian accent:

'Get back all of you! Nobody's taking anything from here until I decide how it's to be distributed. Whoever is hungry will eat, but I'm not standing for idiots...'

Then, he ordered his men to oversee the distribution. He put the locals into a line.

'Let's see, you "old woman" step forward. The rest of you, get in line by the third freight car'. To his comrades, 'Come here, get your rifles readied in case any pest tries it on.'

He then opened a freight car,

'Those who need potatoes...'

He distributed them fairly. Then he handed out vegetables, flour for bread, cans of fruit.

'Are you people satisfied?'

Someone grumbled,

He quickly replied, 'I won't stand for idiots; do you get me? There are shortages in the towns and there are children who are unable to eat. We all have the right to live and you will be alright for a few days. I'll share out what's left, do you get it? We won't touch any of it...'

He was true to his word. Those provisions somewhat alleviated the shortages that were apparent in the neighboring towns, where on certain days it took four hours standing in line to collect two pesetas' worth of foodstuffs. Much of the looting in those days had its origin in the hunger and exasperation of the masses.

Gerardo delivered the remainder to the Provisioning Committee. He requested they reserve the four crates of champagne for his men,

'I want to pop the corks one night, so that these mountain pariahs might drink what the swells drink in expensive hotels.'

Next day they tasked him with capturing a gun which the troops had sited in an extremely dangerous position.

'That gun,' said the chairman of the committee, a noted communist, 'dominates our front lines. Over recent days several comrades have been killed. The gun is causing as much damage as the airplanes.'

Gerardo Monje replied,

'I'll capture that 'little gun' comrade. But I would also beg you comrade to give a little consideration to the workers who are fighting. They sometimes go the whole day without even a mouthful of food.'

The organization was indeed a disaster. Anarchy reigned supreme in the auxiliary services. The miners feared that the struggle could only end in defeat. At that time, it was intensely cold in the mountains. It frequently rained and hailed. The miners out in the open, without blankets or overcoats, stoically bore that unforeseen campaign. Some were almost barefoot, with swollen feet in worn-out boots, or already useless espadrilles. They were sustained by the hope that the revolution was triumphing elsewhere, although the truth is, they were frequently isolated with no more than the odd proclamation from Mieres to renew their faith in the revolution.

There was unprecedented confusion in homes close to the front line, from where the groups were supplied. Women distributed the rations willy-nilly. Some 'ambushers' ransacked storerooms and fled in order to shelter from the gunfire.

Gerardo, who with his small column, was carrying out the instructions of the committees, wished to right those defects. However, it was already too late to put things to rights and bring a modicum of organization to the struggle. In fact, the committees which controlled that front line had allowed the least useful people to join. Swarms of thieves, crooks, women, and little children prowled around it, sowing unrest and anarchy.

The movement had slipped through the hands of its leaders.[17] The committee limited itself to sending out

---

17 Historians have not reached an agreement over whether the Asturian revolution had been a grassroots movement or a top-down one led by the Spanish Socialist Party and to a lesser extent the Communists and Anarchists. It seems, however, that the workers' frustration over decades of poor working conditions compounded with the threat to recent improvements in labor conditions that the economic recession brought with it had been reaching a tipping point. Adrian Shubert explains that "the unrest was general over the coalfields" well before October 1934 (273).

twenty-man patrols, as though it were trying to win such a difficult battle with lightning strikes, taking one position today and another one tomorrow. It lacked revolutionary expertise. On the other hand, there were squads of brave and forceful young miners ready to face death and offer up their lives to the revolution. While the romantic revolutionaries, hungry and barefoot, gave their lives on the barricades, others who were doing nothing, ate their bread and wore their overcoats and shoes, sharing out clothing which the revolutionaries had commandeered.

It was almost futile for Gerardo to submit messages to the committee at Mieres regarding how many topcoats, leathers, waterproof capes, trench coats and shoes remained unissued in stores. When a small batch arrived at the front line, the greater part of the clothing was unserviceable. There were revolutionaries who in order to rest a few hours, without their rain-drenched clothing, lay totally naked among the straw in a hay loft, like a chick in its nest.

On the third morning of Gerardo arriving at the front line, a beautiful day dawned. It was beautiful because the sun gilded the mountain tops; but terrible for those who had to fight against airplanes, rifle, and gun fire. The miners almost preferred rainy, foggy days.

While the sun was soaking up darkness from the mountains, the revolutionaries were taking up positions behind trees and furze bushes, ready to fight the troops and shoot down the airplanes that were dropping bombs and firing machine guns.

Gun fire swiftly alternated with the aerial bombardment. The foothills on the right, running down to Pajares, were in the greatest danger because they were bare of vegetation. The miners who were in the advanced positions were spread out crouching for shelter under any available bush, but they still managed to return fire while watching the bombs fall. When a comrade was hit by shrapnel, there were always a couple of volunteers prepared to carry him on their backs to the ambulance and from there to the field hospital. Sometimes those tragic convoys were spotted by the airplanes; they did not leave their burden but ran with it to where the airplanes could not target them. Some perished in this tragic dodging and ducking to save a wounded comrade.

During clear days, the struggle was too unequal.

When the squadron of airplanes appeared from Pajares that morning, the revolutionaries were still in their burrows on the left slope. The airplanes maneuvered over the positions held by the troops and over those of the red front, without spotting a single revolutionist. When they passed over the houses where the troops were stationed, the miners heard loud shouting,

'Long Live Spain! Long Live Spain!'

They hailed their liberators. Despite being aware of the revolution's misfortune, the miners' hapless siege showed no sign of reaching a conclusion.

Gerardo Monje's men were hidden behind the trees ready to capture the gun. Gerardo blamed himself for not having already attempted that job.

'There are so many things to be done here...'

From time to time an artillery cannonade tore through the air, instantly followed by a muffled explosion. Then the explosions came one after another. It was the signal the airplanes needed; the exploding shells identified the position of the revolutionaries. The gun really served as a spotter.

The troops' offensive lasted all afternoon. The guns

thundered to the sharp accompaniment of the shells. The airplanes, buzzing against the harsh sky, were dropping their shrapnel bombs. All the while, the miners were enveloped in this lethal rain, against which they were almost powerless. It is true that they also had guns, but the ammunition was not time-fused, and their shots were little less than futile.

The only efficient defense against the flyers was rifle fire. On one occasion Gerardo fired; the airplane by its repeated wavering indicated the pilot was wounded. The bomb-aimer however managed to take the controls, but not before the machine began desperate acrobatics, as if to drop. But it soon stabilized and swiftly disappeared behind the Puerto de Pajares.

Gerardo said ironically,

'That's one that won't bother us again. Unfortunately, there are still quite a lot more.'

Casualties among the miners proved it. Despite the danger, a dead man and five seriously wounded had been picked up. One of them had his arm terribly torn by shrapnel; he did not even complain. Another was hit in both legs, leaving only shreds of bloody flesh. He was a worker with a copper-hued face. He said in a weak voice,

'I'm done for... Remember my kids. If we win, you know what to do...'

Later he attempted to get up,

'Give me a rifle...But... I can't... I can't. Let me lie down here. Another bomb will finish me off.'

But then he became intensely pale and died in the arms of a comrade. The miners looked on that already livid face with a mixture of fervor and terror. He was an obscure soldier of Marxism, of whom no one spoke of again.

They buried him on the mountain, close to a stream; for many days, its waters flowed by, mixed with blood.

The miners were awaiting the attack on their positions. But they also were waiting for night before launching an attack, free from airplanes.

'Don't anyone move!' ordered Gerardo Monje.

After four o'clock in the afternoon they saw the troops in extended line move out to attack the revolutionaries' positions, while at the same time the airplanes were dropping their bombs. The guns fired ceaselessly. The revolutionaries let the troops deploy. At less than fifteen hundred meters they unleashed volley fire which caused several casualties. They were the sure shots of hunters.

'Get down!' someone ordered the soldiers.

But the revolutionaries kept calm.

'They can't advance lying down!' said Monje, 'When they get up, let 'em have it!'

The soldiers got up again and began to run keeping low. The Reds' fire stopped them. They were all heading for certain death. They had no choice other than to retire.

Nevertheless, three stragglers were captured by the revolutionaries.

'Don't kill us! We're forced to be here.'

They were taken to the prison compound.

'After all,' said a miner, 'they suffer like us.'

The miners learned from them of the troops' difficult situation during the first days. They could not bury their dead. After four hungry days, rations were thrown to them from the airplanes. If the revolutionaries' guns could have fired using time fuses, they would have been annihilated.

It was vital to capture the 'little gun' that night. Owing

to its strategic position this gun was the most important among those set up by the troops. It dominated the entire northern part of the mountainside. During the hours of aerial bombardment, its shots precisely indicated the miners' position. It was talked of in the rebel towns as the worst enemy machine.

Gerardo Monje, with his group, had promised to silence it. Although other tasks in the struggle had forced him to 'delay,' as he would say in his Buenos Aires slang, that night would be different. He would have to capture the piece as dawn broke. The Reds knew that it was defended by a gun crew in charge of a lieutenant. They also had a machine gun.

In fact, the group launched its reckless venture in the faint light of dawn. The lieutenant must have seen them and doubtlessly, thought to set up an ambush for them. He deployed his men outside their gun position intending to surround the attackers. Just a few were left guarding the gun and they opened fire first, which led the revolutionaries not to suspect an ambush. A few meters from the position they realized that they were caught. Gerardo shouted,

'Comrades, come on, fire!'

The troops pursued them. The lieutenant who was standing up, firing his pistol, shouted in turn,

'It's useless. You'll all die if you don't give up.'

Scarcely had he said this than an accurate shot from Gerardo knocked him over. A sergeant and three soldiers also fell while Gerardo was shouting, 'Come on, comrades!'

They were his last words. Antonio Martín who was firing by his side, saw the rifle fall from his friend's hand as he toppled over without uttering a sound, killed by a bullet to the chest.

Other miners were dead and wounded. Antonio Martín had to organize the withdrawal, while a group of men commandeered one of the troops' machine guns. The gun, however, continued up on the ridge, plotting with the aerial bombers to hammer the armed insurrectionists.

III – The Armored Train

A fireman promoted -Who is 'Red Head'? - The first breakdown-Desertions- 'Red Head' surrenders

In view of the imminent advance of the military forces, the Mieres committee, acting on a request from some youthful revolutionaries, prepared an armored train with men and supplies for Campomanes.

This happened at dawn on the thirteenth day. Despite a week of fighting and the battles for Oviedo being at their height, it was not difficult to find volunteers for the expedition. The train was made up of six cars, which would carry some two hundred men with carbines brought from Oviedo. Another car carried victuals recently requisitioned from the villages, where echoes of the revolution had scarcely reached. They had begun to run short of foodstuffs, among other reasons because total confusion reigned among the supply committees.

Early in the morning the train began to take shape. Everything had to be improvised. The material was jumbled on the sidings, as it had been a week before when the first sparks of the revolution had appeared. Railroad men were nowhere to be seen. Groups of workers checked their homes and were told by the quaking occupants that no one knew anything about them. They asked here and there, 'Who is going to drive the train?' Meanwhile groups were swelling and spreading out along the narrow platform, and through the station offices, spilling out onto the nearby level ground. They were talking loudly, excitedly, recounting brutal details of combat with impressions and rumors from the front line. From time-to-time curses and threats rang out over the muffled drone of snatched conversations.

Finally, by the faint light of the station's lamps, a railroad man appeared between armed miners. He was hatless, extremely agitated and waving his arms about,

'I'll take the train, but I won't answer for it...'

He suddenly halted and said,

'I won't answer for it! I won't answer for it!'

He was a fireman from the Northern Line. They made him climb up onto the foot plate and there, helped by several workers he set to. While some were coupling the cars, others were covering them with armor plating, loading on victuals or furiously discussing what would have to be done. There was no leader. Occasionally, some individual from the committee was tackled by a group of volunteers who raised some problem about the organization of the convoy. The committeeman hesitated, said one thing then another, and in the end slunk away. The volunteers had to sort it out themselves, mouthing insults against 'these incompetent committeemen.'

The most forceful of the volunteers was an almost redheaded youth, indeed everyone called 'Red Head.'[18] 'Red

---

18 "Roxu," "red head" in Bable, the language commonly used in rural areas of Asturias, in the original text. Asturian cultural identity originated side by side Spanish nationalism. Covadonga, the site at which the *hidalgos montañeses* defeated the Berber troops was traditionally considered as the starting point of the Reconquest of Spain by the Christians. Despite a growing interest for Bable and Asturian cultural identity during the eighteenth century when intellectuals like Gaspar Melchor de Jovellanos began to articulate what was to be perceived as Asturian tradition, the Asturian bourgeoisie never fully aligned itself with any form of Asturian nationalism. A *Proyecto de Estatuto Regional para Asturias*, a bill that aimed to acknowledge the cultural and political rights of Asturias as a region was proposed during the Spanish Second Republic, but never garnered enough votes to gain approval. The Francoist regime appropriated As-

Head' went here and there, putting people in the cars, noting down the boxes of ammunition, placing sentries on the platforms. No one knew who he was, nevertheless, everyone obeyed him.

'Hey, who's that kid?'

'I don't know. He must be a communist.'

The fact is that 'Red Head' managed to have the captive fireman promoted by the revolution to engineer, and to get the train moving. It caused something of a thrill among those who were staying and those who were going. The proletarian skill, no matter how basic, like getting a train to move, triumphed at that historic moment. 'Red Head' leant out of one of the windows and shouted at the top of his voice,

'Long Live the Red Army!'

The hurrah was stifled by a long and piercing whistle. The fireman had jerked the whistle which he continued to do for more than five minutes. It was an anguished cry for help rather than a signal for departure. Perhaps that peaceful worker forced to join the rebellion wanted to say goodbye forever, to the wife and children who were so often indifferent to the sound of that train.

The train went well for half an hour; but suddenly a hitch with the boiler brought it to a halt amid protests from the revolutionaries. 'Red Head', who had a carbine hanging from his shoulder and a pistol in his hand, was convinced that the unexpected breakdown was not the fireman's fault. Several mechanics that were on the train made a detailed inspection of the engine, while the rest, without leaving their weapons, lay down close by.

---

turian cultural identity to advance its own agenda making Covadonga into a bulwark of Spanish exclusionary nationalism at the cost of the other national identities in the peninsula.

The delay lasted about three hours. In the end the breakdown was repaired, and the train went on.

Stops had to be made at all the stations on the way. Families were crowded together on the platforms and were exchanging impressions with the revolutionaries. They recounted the destruction caused by the airplanes, the flight of the rich families, and the surrender of the barracks. Men and women with fists raised in the air watched as the train departed.

'U.H.P!' they shouted from below.

'U.H.P.! They answered from the train. But when it left, they all silently moved away, mired in the horror of the revolution.

It was well into evening when the train pulled into the outskirts of Vega de Rey where the forward troops were entrenched at the edge of the railroad track. The troops met the train with volley and machine gun fire. The train answered in kind. But the enemy's fire succeeded in puncturing the metal sheeting around the engine, peppering the boiler. It began to lose steam and water, and the train finally had to stop.

Enemy artillery immediately began to vomit steel. Out of the train came a torrent of swearing and cursing interspersed with the whine of gunfire. Many believed that the engineer had tricked them. A miner wearing a large beret who was firing his carbine from a loophole, jumped down from the car and up into the cabin.

'Get it moving or I'll kill you!' He said pointing his carbine at the unfortunate fireman.

'Red Head' moved the weapon away,

'Don't be stupid. The engine won't go. Look, check it yourself.'

In fact, the engine would not respond to the regulator. The convoy remained stranded there, in the troops' firing line. Suddenly two airplanes appeared, their engines dominating the din of gunfire. In less than a second, they had loosed two bombs which did not explode on the train, but a few meters further on. But shrapnel ricocheted against the armored train, with a metallic echo.

The fireman, curled up in his corner, had given up driving the engine.

'Come here, coward,' shouted 'Red Head' while he was firing. 'We've got to do something. The 'planes are going to finish us off.'

But the railroadman did not move. Then 'Red Head,' in desperation, released the brakes, and saw that thanks to the gradient, the train was moving backward.

'Come here, we're going back down the hill.'

The trembling fireman finally obeyed and took the train to a tunnel between Ujo and Pola de Lena, followed by the airplanes, that were trying to sink their bombs into the train like the talons of twin raptors.

That night the volunteers from the train marched on foot towards the battle front, where for over two days they carried out bitter engagements with troops who were constantly receiving reinforcements from Léon. In fact, it was the last gasp by the miners to breach the enemy line. 'Red Head' wanted to attack the enemy defenses on the sixteenth day. But that approach had already been coldly received. That night the revolutionaries began to desert. On day seventeen, only some fifty men remained with 'Red Head' in charge; they were prepared to resist until the committee ordered their withdrawal. The truth is that by that time there was no committee left. On one pretext or another, the fighters on the front line had gone running into the mountains or were looking for a safe hiding place. They knew that the total failure of the revolution was almost upon them.

'Red Head' exchanged views with his comrades. Almost all wanted to flee.

'Never', shouted 'Red Head.' Besides, we don't know how things are going elsewhere.'

He offered to parlay with the soldiers

'While ever we remain, the revolution isn't beaten.'

But his opinion failed to carry the day. All of them were ready to leave. Then 'Red Head' came up with a crazy decision,

'Well, I'm going to speak to the soldiers. They're proletarians like us...'

There was no way to dissuade him. He shouldered his rifle and made for the enemy position. Soldiers and officers let him come forward, somewhat surprised by the unusual situation. No one knows what happened. His comrades saw him arrive and saw a group form around him. 'Red Head' was talking, wildly gesticulating. Finally, the soldiers took him into their encampment and that was the last anyone saw of him.

IV – In The Hospital

Patricio, the medical auxiliary – The *Guardia Civil's* wife - Tragic search-The Motor Madman-Death of a child.

The wounded from the fighting front at Campomanes[19] and those who had fallen victim to the airplanes along the mining valley were hospitalized in Mieres. A doctor from the *Beneficiencia*, summoned along with others to assist the victims, suggested to the committee the setting up of an Emergency Hospital in the *Escuela de Capatazes*, the only appropriate place for it. Beds and merchandize from stores and private homes were requisitioned; they used the medical material from the clinics and local pharmacies and appointed suitable people, taking revolutionaries, and the bourgeoisie, from here and there. The nurses and auxiliaries were in general people from the non-committed ranks who were offering to volunteer for a task which was not only humanitarian but also had the advantage of keeping them out of harm's way. Those whom we could describe as political, were scarce. A socialist medical auxiliary called Patricio oversaw the set up. He was a reserved, helpful, generous man, who accepted his role without arrogance or pomposity, discharging it as best

19 Campomanes is a narrow access to Oviedo from the south located near the Pajares mountain port twenty kilometers away from Mieres. General Bosch concentrated his troops at Pajares but was unable to defeat the revolutionist guerrillas. On October 14, the Minister of War removed Bosch from his post and sent the Spanish colonial troops led by General Balmes. The arrival of the colonial troops and the realization that the revolution was not taking hold throughout Spain demotivated the revolutionaries that retreated from the southern front on October 18.

he could, given his classist character. There had been many proletarians of this type who in posts of responsibility have behaved without spite or bitterness, strictly adapting their behavior to the duties of the revolution. Others, on the other hand, looked at it differently. Amid the turmoil of war, all the ancestral hatred for the pariahs welled up into their hearts, triggering retaliations and despotism.

Patricio ran the Emergency Hospital with exemplary restraint. The staff found him to be a reasonable man who made their work easier, and the doctors saw in him an energetic and honest leader who did not accept high handed behavior or inequalities. It was the same whether he treated the *guardias* or the insurrectionists, and if he showed any preferences, it was for the women and children who had fallen victim to shrapnel, neutral beings in the terrible and bitter struggle.

Dramatic scenes followed day and night in those wards which days earlier had echoed to the laughter of young men studying the basic technology of mining work. The blackboards, geological maps, set-squares, T-squares, and telemeters were in the corner among blood-soaked gauze and tincture of iodine.

On the first day of the revolution, when numerous wounded had been admitted there, the deranged wife of a *Guardia Civil* from Santullano arrived, her husband having been seriously wounded in the capture of the barracks. She and her son had been evacuated before the revolutionaries had attacked the barracks with dynamite. She had come on foot holding her child by the hand; her skirt was stained with coal dust from the road. They took her to Patricio who gave her permission to search for her husband.

That scene beggars description. The little boy was

clinging to his mother's skirt, crying. With anxiety etched on her face and eyes wide open, she was leaning over the beds of the wounded, trying to see her husband's face from behind the dressings. When she could not clearly make out their faces due to the bandaging and sticking plaster, she called out in a dull voice,

'Ramón! Ramón!'

But Ramón was not there. The woman went from one floor to another, ward by ward, in that fruitless search. Once she realized he was not there, she burst into fearful cries intermittently stifled by her weeping.

'I'm done! I'm! What do I do now with this child, alone in a province where I don't know anyone? It can't be! It can't be!'

Later, in another desperate outburst directed at the workers and staff who were silently listening to her with lowered eyes,

'Kill both of us too! Oh God! How could my husband die without anyone looking after him, without his wife and child at his side!

Those present tried to calm her. There were also wounded who had been provisionally hospitalized in the *Casa del Pueblo*. Perhaps her husband might be there. A worker took her hand and like a blind woman with her Lazarus, she left with her son for the *Casa del Pueblo*.

The route was choked with revolutionaries who were arriving to enlist or returning from detaining prisoners and requisitioning foodstuffs from neighboring villages. The woman eyed them all with suspicion. They were without doubt those who had killed her husband, the implacable enemies of the *guardias*, those who had left her son at the mercy of an orphanage and of misery.

She went through the wards like an automaton. After checking that her husband was not there either, she began to tremble and pale. The frightened child cried,

'Mommy! Mommy!'

With a forlorn look and a foaming mouth, the woman rushed to the balcony railing to throw herself into the yard. The workers managed to hold her back by her skirt when she was already swinging over the void.

In one of the beds was a bandaged boy of between eight and ten years old. Fever had turned his intelligent and sad eyes even brighter. He scarcely made a sound. He meekly watched it all, and when a wounded person moaned or asked for a nurse, the boy stared fixedly at him without blinking. His childish curiosity was whetted even amid such a terrible situation. The tragic impression of those days traced in blood, coupled with the awakening of his consciousness, would certainly never leave him.

The doctors recounted that boy's story, it was one of the most pathetic episodes of the revolution. He certainly did not know what the reason was for the catastrophe which had suddenly destroyed his home. He had come from the Campomanes front. The house where he lived with his parents was in the middle of the battle and they had to leave it; the family lodged in a less dangerous one, although it was exposed to shell fire or bombing. One day, the advanced troops launched a powerful attack during which bombs hit the building where the boy who with many other neighbors had sought refuge. The boy lost a foot and passed out. His father died, and his mother was gravely injured. When the revolutionaries picked them up and carried them on their backs to the road where the ambulance vans were, they were followed by a very low flying airplane which tried to machine gun them. They twice had to leave the wounded so as not to become the bomber's target.

The boy, already in the hospital at Mieres, occasionally asked for his mother. But no one knew what to say. However, his mother died in one of the building's lower wards, without knowing that in a ward on the upper floor her gravely injured child was pining for her.

The horrific scenes ceaselessly followed one after another. One afternoon a woman came in with two little children who had been wounded by shrapnel while she waited in the bread line. Pedro, a white bearded beggar known throughout the valley appeared looking like a martyred saint with feet mangled by shrapnel. That same day, in the courtyard a horrific scene was played out. A quite athletic-looking miner was gnawing at strips of skin dangling from his hands. The nurses and auxiliaries tried in vain to hold him down. He managed to free himself from them and returned to his ghastly autophagy until they managed to subdue him. He suffered repeated attacks of madness.

But the episode that appears like something out of a story by Poe is that of Lucero a young, nineteen-year-old socialist, a chauffeur by profession. The Oviedo committee had sent him to Mieres as the driver for another two revolutionaries who were charged with certain administrative tasks. It was the decisive moment in the fight for the capital. One of those in the car who was obsessed with an imagined pursuit by troops began to shout,

'Faster! Faster, they're coming!'

'Nobody's coming, man!'

'Faster!'

'We're doing eighty; it won't go any faster.'

But the madman was standing up in the car and no matter how much his comrade tried to calm him down, he could not. He took out a cut-throat razor and gave the driver a terrible slash across the neck, saying,

'Take that. You're not going to turn us over to the revolutionaries.'

Lucero stopped the car. The madman ran off through the fields repeatedly shouting,

'They're coming! They're coming! Let's get a move on!'

Lucero, who was mortally wounded in the neck, had to carry on driving to Mieres. He fell down dead in the hospital as they were preparing to treat him.

On another evening, Bautista, a miner who guarded the *Casa del Pueblo*, came in with his wife and his two children. The three were injured by aerial shrapnel. Bautista had his rifle on his shoulder. But as soon as Patricio, the medical auxiliary saw him enter, he was made to leave his rifle outside.

'We have no truck with weapons here.'

He prepared one bed for the woman whose arm had been smashed and others for the children. The child was olive-skinned, with an extremely sweet, round face. His condition was very grave. They had to perform an extremely delicate amputation. When the child came around, he called out,

'Daddy! Daddy! Don't go. Come here, lie down here.'

And he motioned to a place next to him. When his father pretended to lie down, the child's face darkened, his eyes were troubled. Five minutes later he ceased to exist. His father said nothing. He stood rooted while his wife launched into heart-breaking screams.

Moments later the miner left the ward to pick up his rifle again. His sobs rang through the corridors, between the moaning of the sick, the noise of the ambulances and halting, wistful conversations.

V – Langreo

The lost village –The siege of a barracks - Almost impregnable barricades-Executions in the cemetery.

While it was easy to capture government forces in Mieres valley, the same could not be said for Langreo. Langreo is a huge valley on the banks of the Río Nalón. It flows grimy, sluggish, and thick between several somber, huddled villages, randomly scattered on the side of the pitted, tunnel-scarred mountain. The vegetation is stained with coal dust and smoke. Indeed, it is the location of the lost village of which Palacio Valdés[20] spoke. In normal times the coal trains go in and out of the mines, like vermin in their holes. An immense spawn of small towns stretches from Sama as far as Sotrondio. It is where many workers' families live in narrow, dirty, rheumy houses, piled one on top of the other. The mining area is characterized by its lack of housing. Consequently, the workers live cheek by jowl, in the most squalid hovels which, rather than attracting them, drive them away. It is thanks to the taverns and the *Casas del Pueblo* where they meet the civilized world of the cinema, theater, canteen and library, that the miners would learn the rudiments of social solidarity. Poverty and exile daily fed their

20 Armando Palacio Valdés was a Spanish realist novelist and literary critic. His novel *La aldea perdida* presents the miners as a threat to traditional, rural Asturias. His most famous novels, *La hermana San Sulpicio* and *Los majos de Cádiz*, portray Andalusian traditional life. Valdés struggled between his fascination for the romantic portrayal of Spanish life and his understanding that the decline of the Spanish empire entailed the decline of that romantic vision of Spain.

class hatred and sparked rebellion, later stoked by a purely emotive Marxist propaganda[21].

While socialism dominates in Mieres, and the Miners' Union controls the greater part of the organizations, in Langreo communism and anarcho-unionism hold sway. These were grouped into the Trade Union Confederation, which has battled vigorously with the socialist union. Felguera[22], one of the most important towns in the mining valley, is an anarchist stronghold, and it was there, in the huge Duro Felguera workshops, taken by the miners on the first day, where the bombs and the armor plating were made for the trains and trucks used in the siege of Oviedo.

On the morning of 6 October Langreo valley was armed and ready. The committees of the *Alianza Obrera* had circulated orders for a revolutionary meeting and the miners were preparing to take the *Guardia Civil* barracks. They were expecting it to receive reinforcements from Oviedo, therefore, various groups were deployed on the Gargantada road, while others attacked the barracks.

The Red forces of Langreo had rather greater cohesion that those of the Campomanes front line. Communists predominated and readily obeyed their own leadership. In contrast, the anarchists acted on their own volition and on many occasions, ignored the instruction of the committees. In Felguera for example, they attempted to introduce libertarian communism, with the consequent abolition of

---

21 The opening paragraphs of this chapter, a two-paragraph quasi ethnographic analysis of the miners, contrast with the general tone of *Red October*. José Díaz Fernández's narrative is, up until this point, a careful balance of sensationalist propaganda and political reflection aimed to rein in the excesses of the revolution without abandoning its reformist drive. The populist tone of the narration comes to an abrupt halt here and Díaz Fernández provides a brief but incisive diagnosis of the problematic politicization of the miners.

22 Pedro Duro founded Duro Felguera, the first industrial steel mill in Spain, in the mid nineteenth century.

money and the bartering of products within the commune. In the end, it failed. Stores had to be opened and business carried out within the accepted norms required by the circumstances of the struggle.

The revolutionaries were positioned at strategic points on Gargantada; they were soon aware of the arrival of a van with a platoon of *Guardia de Asalto* led by an officer. Fearing a surprise, the *Guardia de Asalto* had their weapons at the ready. Suddenly volley fire from the revolutionaries smashed into the vehicle, which instead of stopping, carried on amid the bullets, with the *Guardia de Asalto* returning fire. Consequently, it reached the bridge and road leading into Sama. But there a wall of revolutionaries forced them to halt, jump out, and take cover behind the van.

The battle was fierce. The *Guardia de Asalto* had two machine guns and swept their enemy's front lines. The most daring miners launched themselves against the van, falling under the enfilading fire never to rise again. At that time the revolutionaries lacked the bombs which hours later would serve to clear the barracks. The *Guardia de Asalto* also suffered losses. One of them, without realizing, had positioned himself in a gap in the railings; a head shot sent him plunging into the river. His body sank under the weight of his cartridge pouches while his comrades, who were unable to help, continued fighting.

Finally, the officer, a youngster, who answered the revolutionaries' entreaties with a grin, decided to make for the barracks, as his situation was becoming ever more precarious. The *Guardia de Asalto* again leapt into the van which set off at full throttle, while its occupants cleared the way with machine gun and rifle fire. The barracks was in a tight spot and welcomed that hoped-for reinforcement. In total the defenders numbered less than one hundred. They were harassed by thousands of revolutionaries who fought throughout the night, simultaneously building barricades with sacks of cement and steel plating brought from Duro Felguera. It turned the barricades invulnerable to all types of fire for many hours.

Next day, the ring round the barracks tightened. Close to midday, the revolutionaries began to attack with dynamite. Furious fusillades by the *Guardia de Asalto* failed to slacken the resolve of the besiegers, who tried out the powerful bombs made by the metallurgists at the Duro Felguera factory. The building was beginning to disintegrate. First, one side collapsed and then the roof began to fall in. Captain Alonso Nart led the defense along with the *Guardia de Asalto* officer but realized that the barracks had to be abandoned. It was a desperate solution; but there was no alternative. The terrible dilemma was whether to be crushed to death or cross the insurrectionists' almost impregnable barricades.

Nevertheless, they broke out. The officers were leading, firing their pistols. Followed by the *Guardia de Asalto*, in skirmish formation, with fixed bayonets, throwing hand grenades. They succeeded in crossing the revolutionist line; but the miners' pursuit was such that the *guardias* were unable to maintain their formation.

'At them! At them!' Shouted the miners as they fired their carbines and shotguns.

The *Guardia de Asalto* fled toward the mountain in small, disorderly groups. Some were no longer young, whereas their pursuers were agile youths, blinded by courage and by blood; they were caught and killed without heeding the instructions of the committees.

The two officers wanted to make for Oviedo at the head of a small detachment. They were alone even before they got to Gargantada. Chased by the revolutionaries, they took refuge in a wayside hut where even there they hoped to put up a fight. It was impossible. The miners, led by a hatless, gabardine-clad youth, hardly twenty years of age, came at them like an avalanche,

'Give up,' shouted the revolutionary.

Captain Nart's only reply was to fire at him, but he missed.

'Argh! Dogs!'

Another miner standing behind him was about to fire at the captain from point blank range. The gabardine-clad boy stopped him,

'Steady! We have to take them alive.'

And so, the two officers were captured. While they were being led towards Sama, decisions were being made about what should be done with them. The gabardine-clad youth said that revolutionary justice could not be delayed. They had to be shot immediately. Whereas a slightly older miner believed that they ought to be handed over to the *Ayuntamiento*, where the committees had gathered,[23]

---

23 The generational gap between the radicalized youth and the older miners that were more willing to negotiate has often been presented as one of the reasons for the multiple divisions within the unions and leftist parties. Union Leader Llaneza complained in the May 15 issue of *El Socialista* that "does not know nor want to know our history, does not understand nor want to understand that they have lived in an extremely unusual time, and that instead of dedicating itself to the conquest of knowledge to raise themselves from their condition of inferiority they let themselves be seduced by the glitter of a flame... which will do away with the virtues which have always been identified with the mine worker" (qtd. In Shubert 275). When labor conditions worsened with the 1929 economic recession, the miners' youth were the first to radicalize their demands unwilling to work in the conditions that the older generation had experienced before them.

'What Committees, they're s....' Said the gabardine-clad youth.

'They should be taken to the cemetery, It'll save work.'

The callous comment was approved without argument.

'As for you,' added the impromptu leader, speaking to the miner who was inclined to clemency,

'If you're not up to it, stay at home...'

The officers realized that death was looming. The captain's face was stained with blood and his tunic torn. But he still had his gloves. He put them on in silence. The lieutenant with his hands tied, followed behind him in another group.

When he saw the cemetery, the lieutenant guessed the insurrectionists' intentions and attempted to free himself and run off. Just then one of his captors fired at him and he fell dead. The captain was shot a few meters away.[24]

The two corpses remained there until the next day and were buried together with other victims. A miner, perhaps the same one who had had compassion for them, commented when they were going down to Sama,

'But they were brave..., that has to be acknowledged.'

Within that very human sentence, beat the true justice of the revolution.

---

24 The assassination of Captain Alonso Nart was documented in the causa 81/1935 in court number 6 of León. José Díaz-Fernández's version of the events differs from that of Manuel Benavides in *La revolución fué así*. Benavides argues that many of the guards under Captain's Nart's command, died as a consequence of an accidental explosion triggered by the guards themselves, and provides no details about the death of Captain Nart himself. José Díaz Fernández uses this episode to highlight the violent acts carried out by the revolutionaries. It is significant that Díaz Fernández does not identify the "gabardine clad youth" as José Gutiérrez Fernández a.k.a. "Pepón de la Campa" who, after being tortured, eventually confessed. Díaz Fernández version of the events suggests that although Captain Nart died at the hands of the revolutionaries, Pepón de la Campa, was not guilty of the crime of which he was accused.

VI – Advance on Oviedo

The Miner and the Capital - The Struggle at San Lázaro - Attack on the *Ayuntamiento* - Ampurdían, the Dynamiter - The Sick Child

While the *Guardia Civil* was being defeated, the miners from the two valleys were gathering in Sama and in Mieres, from where they left in trucks and vans on the way to Oviedo. Many, stirred by danger and eager to get into the firing line, went off carrying *Guardia Civil* bandoliers and rifles. The great, glittering, and attractive city, which many had only glimpsed in quick visits from their miserable mountain homes, exercised an irresistible attraction for the miners. That focus of luxury, comfort, of easy living, drew the miners like a magnet. It was the city to which the engineers escaped to spend the weekends; it was where the mine owners lived, of whom those who hewed coal had only the vaguest notion. In all times, while ever life is organized into social factions, the impulse which will motivate men is the instinct for power. The rough and ready miners wanted to take control of the capital. To their simple souls, political control implied the conquest of everything which until then had been denied them. The word 'revolution' vibrated like an internal motor, it meant above all access to a hitherto forbidden existence. The man with a hard life, the exile from the mean village and the mining district, arrived whirlwind-like to take possession of a new existence. Is it surprising that in resting during the struggle, he should uncork a bottle of champagne in an abandoned store and put on a pair of new shoes?[25]

The first grave mistake of the revolutionaries was to leave open the roads leading to Oviedo. On the sixth day, telegraphic and telephonic communications were cut; but it resulted in vehicles leaving Mieres and Sama being able to reach the office of the *Gobierno Civil* and give notice of the insurrection. It gave time for the defenses to be readied. The first *Guardia de Asalto* vans which left for the valleys were not actually going to stifle the rebellion, rather to hold up the workers so that they would be unable to reach Oviedo as quickly as they planned. If it had not been for this, then Oviedo would have fallen to the revolutionaries on that same day, on the sixth.

The initial skirmishes in Olloniego and Gargantada held them up for a few hours. Although the Oviedo workers were on strike and ready for the fight, there was no armed uprising until the first elements entered San Lázaro. The *Guardia de Asalto* had entrenched there, occupying the best sited and most solidly built houses. The first engagements were extremely violent. As the miners were principally attacking with dynamite there was no way of stopping their advance. After a few hours of very intense fire, the *Guardia de Asalto* were forced to retreat towards Calle de la Magdalena which opens onto the Plaza del Ayuntamiento. Army units had conveniently been entrenched there, they fought for hours without letting the

---

25 The Spanish conservative press had launched a defamation campaign against the miners in the aftermath of the strike accusing them of all kinds of atrocities including the rape of nuns and murder of children. An exhaustive investigation carried out by the government was unable to verify any of these claims. Díaz Fernández aims to provide much needed perspective to understand the acts of vandalism that did take place during the 1934 revolution.

attackers advance. The machine guns which had been sited under the arches, were enfilading the last stretch of Calle de la Magdalena.

The Red revolutionaries could go no farther.

A miner by the name of Feliciano Ampurdián, who handled dynamiting for the vanguard, said that he was going to clear the square. Ampurdián lit the bomb fuses with a cigarette and lobbed them onto the enemy barricades. His footsteps were always marked by horrifying explosions, collapsing roofs, and breaking glass. He was not a man, rather a monster, a mythical Boreas shaking the ground like an earthquake.

That morning, after spending a night in the firing line, Feliciano shouted, 'Volunteers to take the square!'

Within a few minutes, more than a hundred volunteers turned up ready for action. Feliciano set out the plan. In order to reach the *Ayuntamiento* without any delays they were to advance up the street, throwing bombs into the doorways where small *guardia* detachments still held out.

The plan was carried out by some fifty men. There was almost no answer to the explosions, and so they reached the square. The defenders had fallen back on the *Ayuntamiento*, and machine guns were firing continuously from the colonnades, from the balconies, and the church opposite.

The revolutionaries prepared ten of their most powerful bombs and threw them in order to bring down the colonnades. The *guardias* died there enveloped in rubble and chunks of masonry. The machine gunners had to abandon their weapons and withdraw towards Fontán. Elements from Santo Domingo and Campomanes carried on firing. Ampurdián and his men prepared to take the *Consistoriales* building,

'We've got to wipe out those guys up there. Then Oviedo's ours.'

He began to climb the main staircase, but he collapsed, riddled with bullets before reaching the first floor. With blood streaming from his mangled face and mouth he still managed to shout,

'Burn 'em alive!'

The group was consumed by anger and went up firing their carbines. Several *Guardia de Asalto* perished in its defense and others escaped through side doors.

That is how the revolutionaries took the *Ayuntamiento* at Oviedo. In any event, they still took a while to clear the district. Plaza Cimadevilla had to be crossed in a hail of bullets from government forces. The insurrectionists wanted to retrieve the body of comrade Feliciano, but a miner, who tried to cross the square carrying him on his shoulders, was shot down from the balcony opposite. It is strange, that for a couple of days the two corpses lay in the center of the square, in the middle of an enormous black stain, which had been a bloody lagoon. When the troops saw no rebel to fire at, they fired at the two dead men, they were shot many times over the two days.

Next day the Red forces took two neighboring streets. They met stiff resistance from the barracks occupied by the *Carabineros*. Some proposed setting fire to the building and even brought bottles of inflammable liquid to carry out their plan. But women from houses nearby began to shout,

'There are women and children on the second floor!'

So, the miners gave up the idea. But as that enemy had to be destroyed, they devised another plan. The best rifle shots would fire simultaneously at the first-floor windows where the enemy was. The firing would stop the defenders peering out of the windows, while a volunteer miner would rush there to lob several bombs inside. That is how the building was cleared and some *Carabinero* officers killed as they fled. For some days, their bodies also lay in the middle of the street. Passers-by stumbled over them but had no time for sentiment.

The Red forces were finally able to take control of Cimadevilla, where they transferred their headquarters. The committees met in the *Ayuntamiento* from where they issued orders pertaining to the course of the struggle. Having an official building gave heart to the insurrectionists who intensified the siege of the *Gobierno Civil* building. At the same time, various proclamations announced the triumph of the revolution in some provinces and requested one further effort, 'for the total victory of the glorious proletarian revolution.'

Dutor, the socialist, who had been a sergeant, lent a modicum of order to the battling workers. He formed patrols which toured the already conquered districts; he placed Red sentries at strategic points and even prepared a type of intendancy which the Supply Committee acknowledged. In any event, deficiencies had to be overcome by the resolve of those makeshift soldiers who went nights without sleep, and whom no one bothered to supply. However, they rarely stooped to looting, unless they respectfully asked for some provisions in nearby houses.

Residents of the neutral population took refuge in their basements. Revolutionary patrols checking houses and taking the details of their inhabitants found them cringing in their gloomy dwellings. The women prayed. The men understood for the first time that they could not shrug their shoulders in the face of reality, when it appeared suddenly with its sinister claw, to surprise even the most indifferent. The zone occupied by the revolutionaries, where the heaviest fighting had taken place, was exactly where the bureaucrats, people from the liberal professions, pensioners, businesspeople, and petty industrialists lived.

The patrol would arrive banging the door with the butts of their rifles. The menfolk trembled as they opened up,

'Don't be afraid, ladies and gentlemen', said the one who appeared to be the leader. 'We only want the names of those who live here.'

To the peaceful inhabitants of Oviedo, the candle-lit faces of the boy miners, distorted by exhaustion, appeared like monstrous countenances charred by the fires of hell. When they saw that the patrol limited itself to taking notes and left with a 'forgive any bother caused you,' their souls were filled with gratitude. Occasionally the miners requested some food,

'Do you have anything to eat here? We haven't eaten all day.'

The residents rushed to give them stale bread and occasionally spicy pork sausage and tinned food,

'Thanks very much. There are lots of us and food's scarce.'

One afternoon a patrol composed of just four miners called at a house in Calle de la Magdalena. The owners had taken shelter on the first floor. Among them was a woman with her sick child. Her soldier husband was evidently fighting at the Santa Clara barracks. The child who had a high fever was constantly asking for water.

'Is the child sick?' One of the workers asked.

'Yes. He's been like this for a week.' Answered his tearful mother. 'I don't know what to do with him.'

'And hasn't a doctor seen him?'

'The one who came hasn't been for three days. Oh, my God, what will become of me?'

'Don't worry. I'll bring one of our doctors.'

They finished their searches and left. A quarter of an hour later, the soot-blackened boy with the red jersey, turned up with a young revolutionist doctor.

'Let's see comrade. Have a good look at the little fellow... He's not to blame for the revolution.'

The doctor examined the child by flickering candlelight. The thermometer registered a fever of 40 degrees centigrade.

'How long is it since this little child ate anything?'

'The milk ran out yesterday. I haven't been able to give him more than a little bread soup.'

'You need to give him milk or phoscao[26], three times a day. You need to get some from the warehouse where they deliver the foodstuffs.'

The exhausted, red-eyed women could only cry. Other women in the house consoled her.

The miner promised to bring her some milk for the little sick child,

---

26 Chocolate powder drink. Cocoa was initially brought from America by the Spaniards and quickly became a luxury drink. The import of Guayaquil cocoa in the eighteenth century helped to lower the price of chocolate and make it popular among the middle classes. In the nineteenth century, Spain started importing cocoa from Equatorial Guinea, at that time a Spanish colony. The colonial dimension of the cocoa trade was often used in marketing materials to emphasize the exotic nature of the product. The Catalan company Nutrexpa, that acquired Phoscao in 1964, became infamous for its television and radio commercials touting the virtues of cocoa as the drink of the Tropical black man. Díaz Fernández could not have been unaware of the colonial echoes that resonated during the repression of the Asturian miners by the Spanish Foreign Legion and the *Regulares* of the Spanish colonial army in Morocco.

'Keep calm. The child won't go without food. I'll see to that myself.'

For two days, he was in effect, supplying that family with condensed milk procured with the coupons which the Supply Committee had allocated him. But on the third day the doctor arrived alone. The child was getting better and was already out of danger,

'And where's your comrade?' The mother asked. 'He hasn't come around today.'

The doctor who was already on his way out replied,

'He won't be coming back. They killed him this morning in the Plaza de la Escandalera.'

VII – Oviedo In Flames

The Torching of a Bank - The Blowing up of the University - The Ambulant Inquisitor - The Tragic Mask - The Prisoner-Facing the Committee

The revolutionaries occupied the university by surprise on the night of the seventh day. It was an essential position from which to mount an attack on the Banco Asturiano, which troops had fortified with the object of blocking access to the *Gobierno Civil* building.[27]

When Peña learned that they had taken the university, he sent a message, 'Be careful of what you do. Try not to damage anything.' The university had actually been earmarked as a holding area for prisoners. But the battle with the bank's defenders forced the revolutionaries to use the turret as a firing point. Government forces fired on that redoubt which was soon demolished by machine gun fire. Several workers died out there in the open firing their rifles. The revolutionaries, exasperated by these losses, hurled cans of gasoline through the windows of the bank eight or ten meters away. Then they threw bombs wrapped in cotton and soaked in gasoline. The exploding

27 The looting of the Banco Asturiano and later the Banco de España in Oviedo led to confrontations between the leader of the miners Ramón González Peña and some of the revolutionaries. González Peña ordered to put a halt to the revolt after the Banco de España was looted but was ignored by the revolutionaries. Interestingly, JDF does not mention González Peña once. A pamphlet titled "Los crimenes de la reacción española" produced by the Spanish section of the Comintern agency International Red Aid (SRI) and published on the one-year anniversary of the Asturian revolution, accused López Ochoa without evidence, of blowing up the safe of the Banco Asturiano and stealing its contents.

bombs ignited the gasoline, setting the building alight, and causing it to spread over the whole block. The few embattled troops there had to get out quickly. The flames set a *guardia*'s uniform ablaze; he was burnt to death as his companions were forced to leave him to save themselves.

This happened on the tenth day. The flames shot more than three meters above what had been the roof of the Bank. From San Lázaro, the city looked like an immense torch. In the dead of night, the fires provided the only light. The guns thundered to the almost constant sound of rifle and machine gun fire. The hammering of gunfire, merged with explosions and collapsing buildings, produced a savage howl as though it were not a human thing. The atmosphere was dominated by a dense reek of gunpowder, of gases mixed with the smell of the filthy, detritus-filled streets, of unburied corpses, and of congealed blood.

That was war, perhaps it was more horrible than war because it lacked the army's rigid organization, and above all, it highlighted the tragic improvisation, the surprising absurdity of not knowing at any time what was going to happen.

Next day, the university was blown up, it is not known whether it was the revolutionaries' dynamite or the airplanes' bombs. One claims that an aerial bomb dropped onto a laboratory and caused the fire. Another maintains that it was an accidental explosion of dynamite which the revolutionaries had stored there.[28] What is certain is that

---

28 The pamphlet published by the Spanish Government accused the revolutionaries of blowing up the university in their attempt to take control of Oviedo. According to the account of the events made by General López Ochoa in his war diary *Campaña militar en Asturias en octubre de 1934* suggest that the revolutionaries played no role in the bombing of the university.

the ancient house where 'Clarín'[29] lectured his classes ('Clarín' and his opposites, the time-serving teachers) completely collapsed, becoming a jumbled mound of stones and rubble. Only the statue, the symbol of its founder, Archbishop Valdés[30], the inquisitor-general, remained unscathed. Apparently, that fire was a friend of his from inquisition days and respected his effigy.

The La Vega Weapons Factory was besieged right from the start. It was furiously attacked by the revolutionaries, but the defenders held out. On the ninth day, Sergeant Vázquez, who commanded the groups, ceased firing in order to organize the assault.[31]Neither did the defenders fire even though they saw the Reds grouping for a fresh attack. It was being said amongst the revolutionaries that there were only dead bodies inside. Two of the besiegers, long-time workers from the factory, volunteered to enter and after a reconnaissance estimate the number of its defenders.

They did just that. And they also seized a machine gun. It appeared that the soldiers were absolutely exhausted,

---

29 Leopoldo Alas (1852-1901), alias Clarín, was a Spanish novelist and one of the most prominent representatives of Spanish naturalism. Although, Clarín was born in Zamora, most of his novels take place in Asturias. His most famous novel, La Regenta, describes the oppressive world of the Oviedo bourgeoisie at the end of the nineteenth century. Clarín was greatly influenced by Krausism and a convinced republican. His journalistic articles criticizing the Spanish monarchy and the Catholic church were a staple of the Spanish democratic press of the time.

30 Fernando de Valdés Salas (1483-1568) was a General Inquisitor and President of the Council of Castile. Valdés held many important positions within the Catholic Church, being the Bishop of Oviedo in 1532. As General Inquisitor, Valdés drafted an index of forbidden books and prosecuted Moriscos (Muslim converts to Christianity) as well as Erasmists and Lutherans. Valdés led the trial against Bartolomé de Carranza. Archbishop of Toledo, who was eventually absolved.

31 The De La Vega Weapons Factory founded in 1856 was, with the Trubia Weapons Factory, one of the first industrialized weapons factories in the region. The availability of raw materials like iron and coal made the region a highly suitable location for this type of industry. The weapons factories contributed greatly to the local economy and to the demographic boom that the region experienced in the second half of the nineteenth century.

and seeing that the revolutionaries had ceased to attack, the majority had fallen asleep. Very early next morning, the workers redoubled their efforts and were already up to the windows of the building. The soldiers finally abandoned their weapons and fled through the rear windows which gave onto the Vasco-Asturiano railroad line. Some were unable to escape; they were rounded up and led to the hospital, wounded and hungry.

From that moment on the revolutionaries had large stocks of armaments. Heavy weapons, rifles and carbines were handed out. But afterwards the ammunition they had wasted with the same liberality as they had wasted medical supplies and food stuffs, began to run low. The miners believed that Spain would already have fallen into the hands of the workers by that time and were awaiting comradely reinforcements which never arrived.

Meanwhile, fighting was taking place in Calle Uría, in Campo de San Francisco, and in Plaza de la Catedral. A group of revolutionaries had sited a gun in the grounds of the hospital to bombard Calle Uría, which was still held by the troops. On the ground, under the branches of a leafy tree, were more than two hundred 10.50 mm shells. They had dug in the gun and a metallurgist was to be its gunner. After the gun was in place the gunner asked,

'What do we do now?'

'Shoot.' Answered one of the group.

'But first we need to know where those swindlers are.'

'They're down Calle Uría in the Park.'

'Oh! Then we'll have some good shooting...'

'Then, fire!' shouted the gunner.

The gun was loaded and fired over open sights. But no explosion was heard. They fired again but heard nothing.

'How come we don't hear the explosion?' One of them asked.

'Because we don't have time fuses.'

It was like throwing a rock into the air, which with luck, might hit an enemy on the head.

But the shots were very quickly answered from Campo de San Francisco by rifle and machine gun fire. The bullets whistled over their heads. There were about fifty revolutionaries who got behind a wall to return fire, as the gun went on firing blind.

Then the revolutionaries came up with the idea of attacking Campo de San Francisco from the corner of Calle Marqués de Santa Cruz. They made their own way crawling between the trees to the agreed forming up point.

They began shooting from there, but the troops' superior fire power caused many casualties. Two revolutionaries attempted to rescue a wounded comrade from under fire. One of them was hit in the face by a bullet while trying. The wound was not serious, but he was bleeding a lot. Nevertheless, they managed to get the wounded man away. Meanwhile two more men were wounded. Then they all withdrew. The man with the facial wound was incensed,

'But comrades are we going to abandon the position? Stay put everyone even if we all die!'

In a fit of rage, he put his hand to his face and made a frightening mask with his own blood. It was the living image of the horror of war. He carried on shouting,

'Comrades, all of you, come to me!'

But no one took any notice of him. A van loaded up the wounded to transport them to the hospital. While the van parked in the next street, was starting up, the man with the bloody mask was again wounded by a shot to the chest. Several of the comrades lifted him up and loaded him onto the van. This time he was dead.

The troops at Campo de San Francisco captured a miner who had recklessly got too close to them. This often happened. A kind of rivalry to see who was the boldest was engendered among the revolutionaries. Just as in their mountain fairs they often took part in such primitive tournaments where young women were well used to them firing off pistols in their honor, now the miners brought their daring brawls to the revolution. One of them broke the 'record' for recklessness but paid for it with his life; he was the one involved in the fighting with a group of *Guardia de Asalto* on the roadway, who leapt into a van, and let go of the brake while throwing his bombs. He put most of the *Guardia de Asalto* out of commission but died in the act.

The miner who reached the redoubt held by the troops was spotted by a sentry and immediately captured. He was taken under guard to an officer who interrogated him. The miner showed great calm. It contrasted with the noticeable unease among the small government encampment.

'What have you come here for?' The captain asked him.

'I'm not going to lie to you,' answered the worker. 'I wanted to find out how many of you there were.'

'But don't you realize you're risking your life?' the officer quickly replied.

'I already know that. But you are also risking your lives. You'll now take your revenge on me.'

The captain thought that it would be best to take advantage of the miner's calm, self-control. 'I already know that you have lots of weapons. All of those from La Vega. Roughly how many of you are there?'

'Oh, I don't know. Every day more arrive to join in the fight.'

'I'm aware that you already have guns.'

'And machine guns.'

'How many guns do you have?'

'I can't be certain. I know of three.'

'And machine guns?' stressed the captain, who appeared worried by that news.

'In my sector alone, there are more than ten. We've taken some from you.'

'But the guns, you don't know how to use them.'

'Come on! Workers who are better gunners than you have come from Trubia.'

'Right, and what do you think you're going to do with Oviedo? You're destroying it.'

'What we want to do is take it. The committee says it's trying to do as little damage as possible; but it must be taken. And as to how will it be taken... Have no doubt we will take it, come what may.'

'But we won't let you.'

The revolutionist shrugged his shoulders.

'Besides, reinforcements are coming from other provinces.'

The officer began to laugh; it was intended to sound sarcastic,

'From other provinces... But it's completely failed... There's only you left. You've got radios. Haven't you heard that it's all over? In Madrid, it was nothing more than a few desultory shots.'

'Yes. That's what they say on the radio. But that's to mislead us.'

'Very good. I'll shoot you here and now.'

The miner stood looking at him, 'You can do that, because I'm in your power, but don't think that this is the end of the revolution.'

'You've all been deceived. What do you think the revolution is?'

'Well, the revolution... It's something that will never end, even if you finish us all off.'

The captain stamped crazily.

'Don't you understand that this is drivel? You won't take Oviedo. You won't take it. Do you hear?'

A few meters further away a group of officers and *Guardia de Asalto* overheard the strange conversation. The situation must have been difficult for the defenders. The captain called two lieutenants over and for some minutes the three of them held a lively discussion.

The captain returned to the prisoner and said to him,

'Look, I'm going to let you go free because you're brave[32], but on condition that you take a message to the Committee. Tell it our news that the revolution has failed throughout Spain; the best thing to do is to withdraw without causing further damage, and we promise not to take reprisals. I'm taking personal responsibility for this. But I believe your committee doesn't know what's happening in the rest of Spain. Otherwise, our airplanes will flatten you. And now, you can go.'

The miner, whose rifle had been taken from him, left the redoubt and by keeping clear of danger, made his way to the *Ayuntamiento* where the Committee, the first one

---

32 Throughout *Octubre Rojo*, Díaz Fernández subverts the male bravado that characterized accounts of the 1934 strike in which one side would question the masculinity of the other. In Díaz Fernández's account, courage is not used to differentiate the brave revolutionist from the effeminate civil guards (as many pamphlets of the time would), but rather to highlight the human connection between revolutionaries and the armed forces.

under the U.H.P., banner was in session. At that very moment, the committee members were holding a heated discussion with the leader of the Gijón trade union movement, José María Martínez[33], who was to die rather mysteriously, a few days later.

Martínez was a tall man with a florid face and intelligent eyes. Struggling against the anarchist current within the Gijón workers' organization, he had managed to form the *Alianza Obrera* with socialists and communists. He was asking the committee for weapons to fight the naval and local forces who had defeated them the previous day, after having bombarded the fishermen's district. But the Committee claimed it could not release weapons or ammunition until Oviedo was taken by the revolutionaries. Everything was needed to put pressure on the defenders of the city who continued to hold out despite the efforts of the besiegers. José María Martínez insisted,

'If you don't give me weapons, Gijón will be wide open and the troops will finish you off.'

'Once Oviedo is taken,' answered the committee, 'nobody will enter Asturias. We already have the province under our control.'

'A province with an open door. If you don't control the ports, you have nothing.'

Basically, what they were already discussing was the

33 José María Martínez (1884-1934) was the founder of the first miners' anarchist trade union "El despertar del minero" (the miners' awakening). After living in exile in Portugal for some time escaping from the police as a result of organizing numerous strikes and confrontations with the administrators of the mines, Martínez returned to Gijón in 1916. He advocated for the alliance of the anarchist Comité Nacional del Trabajo (CNT) and the socialist Unión General de Trabajadores (UGT) in the mining sector. He continued to defend the strategical value of an alliance of Anarchists and Socialists during his life for which he was harshly criticized by Buenaventura Durruti and Eusebio Carbó, both of them prominent leaders of the CNT.

predominance of workers' groups in the revolution. The socialists considered it suicidal to hand weapons to the anarchists who completely lacked control in Gijón.

Martínez took his leave with a threat,

'I'm going to La Felguera and there I'll find men. If the revolution fails, it will be because of you. But we'll hold you to account.'

When the miner sent by the captain at Campo de San Francisco appeared in front of the committee, they hardly took any notice of him,

'Bah, bah,' said one of the leaders. 'That's just nonsense. They're trying to bamboozle us. Don't take any notice of them. The revolution is winning.'

Several hid a wry smile which was not lost on the miner. Then they asked him for details about what he had seen during his brief arrest. The youngster accounted for all he was asked without concealing his conversation with the officer and that man's worries about the weaponry held by the workers.

Campo de San Francisco was captured on the following day. Large groups of revolutionaries with machine guns launched themselves against the defenders. At the same time an armored truck which had been fitted up at the Trubia Factory[34] drove along Calle Uría, vomiting lead through its loopholes. The bullets whipped through the almost leafless branches. The birds in the little zoological park, the ducks and doves flapped here and there crazed, and terrorized. The paths where 'Clarín' had strolled, in search of the footsteps of 'La Regenta,' were strewn with rubble and shell casings.

---

34 The Trubia Weapons Factory was one of the first companies to produce arms industrially.

The *Guardia de Asalto* captain and some of his men were captured and locked up in the *Teatro Principado*. On the way, he was clearly recognized by the miner who had been his prisoner the day before. They both looked at each other without a word. In fact, that was the moment the officer got the answer to his message. But the miner, who was just a soldier of the revolution, knew how to thank the captain for his behavior. He did it in a very simple way by telling the Red guards at the theater to treat the prisoner with as much basic gratitude as they could muster. Having taken Campo de San Francisco, an entire area of the capital was under proletarian control. The revolutionaries were constantly being sniped at from a building called *La Casa Blanca*.[35] The revolutionaries raked the roof with artillery fire and demolished it in a few minutes.

On the twelfth day, a *Guardia de Asalto* major attempted to retake the Park. He came out of Santa Clara Barracks with less than one hundred men, and quickly deployed his force in Plaza de la Escandalera, crossed Calle Uría, and came out in the direction of the Park,

'Forward, boys!'

But it was in vain. Within moments, he fell with a bullet wound to his foot. Some *guardias* died there. Amid deadly fire, they were forced to retire on the barracks with their dead and wounded.

The main body of the government forces were fighting from the shelter of Pelayo Barracks. From the beginning, there were heroic leaders who fought with extraordinary presence of mind. But there were others, who when discussing the seniority of those present, and who would take

---

35 Art Deco building designed by architect Manuel del Busto that was built in 1929 in Oviedo's downtown area.

responsibility for its defense, flopped down into armchairs declaring,

'You only die once. I'm not going.'

The barracks, which were in communication with their airplanes by means of large lettering on the rooftop, had been under siege for three days. The workers even attacked it with dynamite. The volunteers would constantly go out to throw their bombs or die under fire from inside the barracks. On the twelfth day, the barracks under pressure from Dutor[36], was in a desperate situation. Despite gunfire from the besiegers, a pilot dropped food supplies there, and was able to read the distressing message written on a rooftop sheet, 'We only have enough ammunition to last until tomorrow.'

Someone proposed sending a truck full of dynamite against the barracks, after the style of a trebuchet. There were volunteers who would carry out the plan even though they knew it would mean certain death. Peña opposed such an extreme option, besides he understood that it was already too late. The revolution had failed in Spain.

Plaza de la Catedral was the place where they fought with real fury. From the first day, Peña had begged the gunners from Naranco,

'Don't fire on the Cathedral! It would be very bad for the revolution.'[37]

---

36 Francisco Martínez Dutor, sergeant in the Spanish Protectorate of Morocco, became a member in the UGT trade union and the Spanish Socialist Party (PSOE) after returning to Spain. After participating in the Asturias revolution, he escaped to France and eventually Russia.

37 *La revolución de octubre en* España, the official account of the events of October 1934 published by the Spanish government, accused the revolutionaries of burning the Holy Chamber of the Cathedral intentionally. In an article published in *La Veu de Catalunya* on October 26, Catalan writer Josep Pla commented: "The events in Asturias are incomprehensible. They defeat any attempt at a rational or logical explanation." Manuel Benavides argues in *La revolución fue así: (octubre rojo y negro)*

But the Cathedral had become a strategic position for the revolutionaries in their defense of the *Gobierno Civil* building. A worker said to Peña,

'You don't want to fire on the Cathedral. But the Cathedral is firing on us.'

It had to be attacked with rifle fire. Afterwards dynamite was used. An army lieutenant fought there with soldiers and *Guardia Civil*. They had positioned several machine guns in the small turrets of the Cathedral, from where they blocked the passage of the revolutionaries who fell without being able to cross the square. At the time, who could possibly appreciate attacking a XIII century church, a gothic marvel, its stones weather-beaten for seven centuries? The miners did not understand archaeology or history, and during those hours the terrified scholars were in their dark cellars, while the gun thundered, and machine guns rattled from the tower. That tower had for centuries witnessed the peaceful passage of clouds, of swifts and clerics. Its stones alone bore witness to the beginning of nationhood, even before they were formalized by architects; they felt the passage of the Cid when he came to marry Doña Ximena, the daughter of the Count of Oviedo.

The revolutionaries saw only an enemy position there. Bodies were strewn on the flagstones of the square which ordinarily feel the light step of Oviedo women. Blood coursed towards the saintly doors against whose ironworks bullets constantly ricocheted. It was a bomb thrown

---

that the revolutionaries debated whether to attack the cathedral or not because of its historical value but concludes that the Catholic Church had done little for the workers and hence the cathedral did not deserve to be saved (284).

at the defenders of the Cathedral which blew in the *Cámara Santa* which in the IX century, Alfonso the Pure, had ordered built to guard the Christian relics from Palestine, and then hid them from the Moslems. These other illustrious stones of the Holy Chamber were certainly not unduly intimidated by the thunder of dynamite. The truth is that some of the oldest are contemporaneous with Don Ramiro, that Christian king who to safeguard his throne, ordered the eyes of his adversaries to be gouged out before sentencing them to death at the stake in company with all their children and relatives. In Asturias, civil war and repression have notorious antecedents.

VIII – The Country Doctor

Health Needs - The Thieves of Calle Fruela - An Airplane Hunts a Car - 'That is not the Password.'

The hospitals were short of medical supplies and messengers were frequently arriving from Langreo and Mieres requesting medication be sent to them. The committee nominated a young doctor to inspect the services. No sooner had this doctor heard news of the revolution than he had left his position as principal of the rural council to take part in it. He was a fair-haired boy, with an optimistic air, who alternated carrying a rifle with first aid treatment. He had taken part in the attack on the Armaments Factory and could always be seen in the places of greatest danger. He belonged to the Young Socialists, and in remote mountain villages, in company with a communist schoolteacher, was propagating Marxism well before October. Peasants who could hardly read and until then did not know that Russia existed, knew about Lenin and Stalin, and were aware 'from what the doctor said,' of Soviet reforms.

This doctor, Ramón Tol[38], was one of the intellectuals who fought in the revolution. His Marxism was purely starry-eyed; but he dreamt of a new and more just world. When he met villagers working the land or looking after animals, he would call to them,

38 We have very little information about Ramón Tol. He is described as a rural doctor by Bernardo Díaz Nosty in his book *La comuna asturiana: la revolución de octubre de 1934* who, in turn, refers to Díaz Fernández's account as evidence of Ramón Tol's existence and participation in the revolution.

'Do you know that tenancies will come to an end? The land is going to be yours.'

The villagers were skeptical, but deep down they thought that something unusual was happening when the doctor, a young gentleman, was talking like that. These villagers loved him dearly. Because the doctor not only went with them to the *Ayuntamiento* and the Court House to resolve issues and argue with court clerks on their behalf, but also did not charge them for his visits, even though he would disappear for weeks on end when he went to the capital. After the revolution, these peasants hid Ramón Tol and led him on horseback over the mountain to Galicia from where he entered Portugal.

Thus, Ramón Tol was commissioned by the committee to inspect the health services. A comrade drove him to Langreo in one of the requisitioned cars, while in Oviedo the fighting was still going on. Tol already felt that the movement was in decline, but he encouraged everyone by his own example. He had gone four days without sleep, his hair was tangled, his trench coat stained with blood and his shoes filthy with sloshing around in the blood-stained mud. That morning numbers of miners had begun to desert. The car crossed the deserted Plaza del Fontán with its broken stalls and icy arcades. Two characters with rifles over their shoulders were busy looting boxes of shoes from an apparently abandoned shoe store.

The doctor put his head out of the window and spoke to them,

'Hey, is this how you fight?'

The two petty thieves stared at the doctor but did not dignify a reply neither did they stop their work.

The driver made half-hearted excuses for them,

'The *guardias* are looting as well. If it wasn't for what they scrounge there, no one would be doing any fighting.'

Tol replied,

'But we Marxists don't do that.'

Many miners were returning home. It was raining in torrents and the road was a quagmire. Some workers stopped the car to get a ride. The doctor took the first two who were injured and exhausted. They had gone a week without rest. They were from Sotrondio, if it had not been for that chance car, they would have been forced to make a roundabout journey and expend hours on the road. However, they were thinking about returning to the front. They were going home to recover and would return to carry on the fight. Tol cheered them up and when he reached Sama, he requested help for them. However, it was not possible as everyone was asking for it; the elements of resistance had been exhausted.

Ramón Tol searched out the committee and left for the hospital at Duro Felguera. In the operating theater, a surgical team was amputating the leg of a wounded *guardia*. The surgeon's rubber gloves were dripping in blood.

It was there that the doctor saw how scarce medical supplies were. Iodine and dressings had been squandered; there were not enough beds or special dietary foods. The revolutionaries had not counted on that number of wounded from both sides. Tol made a list of that hospital's needs and promised to send it, without being very sure that he would find enough in Oviedo.

The same thing happened in Mieres. But there the squalor in the emergency hospital would fill the calmest soul with terror. Tol understood that it would be impossible to meet the demands of those committees, and once again saw that they had failed to anticipate a series of requirements which were an essential part of the struggle.

They had to drive back to Sama with a gravely wounded man who could not be operated on in Mieres. But when Tol wanted to return to Oviedo by car, they told him he would have to go by way of 'El Berrón.' The other roads were unsafe. The revolutionaries had blocked this road felling leafy trees along its length and blowing down some retaining walls with dynamite. The trees had been uprooted with a packet of dynamite tied to their trunks. Time was at a premium. There were few men available as they were concentrated at the battle front, so they had decided to put trees in place of sentries.

They had scarcely arrived at the blocked part of the road when Tol's car was stopped,

'Halt,' shouted an imperious voice.

'U.H.P!'

The Red guards checked the car and began putting planks down across a large ditch some meters deep. The driver refused to cross over that improvised bridge, but the doctor urged him on,

'You're not scared of bullets, yet you're scared of crossing over where the others have.'

The car finally moved forward and rapidly set off towards Oviedo. But suddenly a relatively low-flying military airplane appeared and on spotting the car, dropped a bomb intending to destroy it. The shrapnel missed the car. But the airplane immediately prepared to attack again. The driver drove the car into a chestnut grove, its passengers leapt out and ran toward the foot of a thick chestnut tree. Shrapnel from the second bomb lodged in a nearby tree trunk.

Ramón Tol was sorry he had not brought his rifle to shoot at the airplane. Nevertheless, he fired with his pistol, even though he knew it would be useless.

'At least,' he thought to himself, 'I've done my duty in having a go at the enemy, even though it didn't work.'

On entering Calle Uría two armed sentries stopped the car. Tol gave the password,

'U.H.P!'

One of the boys began to laugh,

'It's not the password comrade. That was this morning's.'

'That's what the committee gave me. I don't know any other.'

'Well, that committee has gone and they're looking for it. We have no choice but to detain you.'

'But I'm a socialist! I've come to inspect the hospitals by order of the committee.'

'Look, we're going to take you to Herrero's villa. You'll be able to work it out with the organizers there.'

One of the sentries climbed into the car and ordered the driver to carry on to Plazuela San Miguel. The new committee, composed of communists, was meeting there in the villa belonging to the banker Herrero.'

'Fine,' said the chairman, 'This comrade is known.'

And then turning to Tol, he said,

'I take it that you'll place yourself at the disposal of the new committee.'

The doctor replied, 'I'm always at the disposal of the revolution.'

'Well grab a rifle.'

'Alright. But the other committee charged me with the inspection of hospitals.'

'Fine. That committee carries no weight.'

'They're short of the most basic things in Sama and Mieres.'

'There's nothing to be done comrade. Now it's all about capturing Oviedo and proclaiming the Workers and Peasants Republic in Asturias.'

IX – Prisoners And Fugitives

A Serious Moment - The Bank Manager - International Treaties - Panic in the Prison - A Prisoner's last Hour.

The prisoners had been held at different sites. The main locations were in the *Teatro Principado*, the University, and the Institute. There were no detention orders against anyone. They were spontaneously arrested by workers or captured in the thick of battle. The revolutionaries took them to the *Ayuntamiento* and there the committee had authorized their detention. There were priests, magistrates, a bank manager, and soldiers from the La Vega Factory. Teodomiro Menéndez, who had been in the *Ayuntamiento* from the first day, took an interest in the prisoners. The committee promised to respect them. It is true that the fighters' blind impulses were darkly fueled by personal vengeance, and that several were shot by the mobs.

The bank manager was detained at a critical moment. The Plaza del Ayuntamiento was packed with revolutionaries when an airplane suddenly emerged. It dropped two high explosive bombs and then made off before riflemen had time to reply. The panic and confusion it caused are indescribable. Some of those present were blown to pieces. Torn limbs, smashed skulls and lumps of bloody flesh were thrown against the columns of the arcade. Many men fled in terror and others, ashen faced, crowded together in the doorway of the *Consistoriales*, fearing fresh explosions. After a few minutes had passed, the revolutionaries recovered and gathered in groups under the arcades, to talk about what had happened. That event was so shocking that a committee spokesman had to go down to speak to the comrades. They had to redouble their efforts to take Oviedo. One of the proclamations published later, announced that to prevent aerial attacks, there would be imminent aid from revolutionaries in the rest of Spain.

'If only we had airplanes!' could be heard repeatedly directed at the Reds.

The bank manager was detained that morning after the bombardment. When they took him to the *Ayuntamiento*, he was insulted by a squad leader,

'They're bandits! They don't abide by international treaties!'

The detainee did not fully understand the connection the revolutionaries had made between international politics and what was happening in Oviedo. But afterwards he deduced that apparently, aircraft bombs had also fallen on the hospitals and on the non-combatant population.

Despite the Reds' evident annoyance, the committee conducted itself without violence or animosity toward the prisoner. It ordered that he should be locked up in the Institute and treated with respect.

The prisoners were in one of the classrooms. They had neither beds nor blankets because the mattresses had been used as barricades for the fighting. Red guards were watching the doors. Twice a day they were brought canned food and a little bread. Actually, they had been short of food for the last few days, and the prisoners had only eaten some cookies. But the fighters ate little more. One afternoon the bank manager was peremptorily called out,

'Citizen, to testify!'

The other prisoners believed that the executions were beginning. They tearfully said goodbye to the presumed victim. One of the imprisoned priests blessed him. When the banker went out, they all fell quiet, silently praying.

The pallid-faced banker followed behind the man who had called him out and who led him to another room where the warden was. He was a socialist from Oviedo whom the banker knew by sight. On the table were a large jug of milk and a box of cookies.

'Sit down, Don Nicanor. Let's have something to eat.'

Nicanor felt deep down that having been sentenced to death, they were about to give him his last meal. His answer was not a joke,

'I must tell you that I'm really not hungry...'

'And you've gone without food for two days? Sit down man, sit down! We're certainly not as bad as they say.'

The banker sat down, slightly more in control of himself. He did not believe that the Reds had attained the refinement of extending invitations to those presumed to be shot.

'Well, this morning,' continued the acting-warden, 'Some youngsters from Sama brought me these cookies, and I told them I was going to invite Don Nicanor, as that poor little man was having a bad time.'

'Then you didn't call me to testify?'

No, Goodness no. It's just for form's sake.'

The banker suddenly developed an enormous appetite. In between diving into the cookies, he took large swigs of milk; he could not get enough.

It pleased the jailer who felt the time was right to urge him to accept the new state of things.

'We need intellectuals Don Nicanor. You must join us.'

'But I don't know anything other than banking, and you're going to abolish money.'

'Well, we'll have to see about that.'

'Besides, I believe that you're failing. It's very difficult to restructure a society.'

'Don't believe it, Don Nicanor. Look what's happening in Russia.'

The banker thought it imprudent to continue a discussion, which in those circumstances, could become very risky. After appeasing his hunger, he remembered the lot of his fellow-prisoners,

'My Goodness! I'd like to take something for the other prisoners.'

'Don't worry, I'll send what's left so that you can share it out.'

'Now have a cigar, Don Nicanor.' He said holding out a splendid Havana. 'I've kept this one for you.'

When the banker returned to his companions, he got a most anxious welcome. He was puffing clouds of smoke, almost happily.

'But what's happened Don Nicanor?' the priest asked him. 'Aren't they going to shoot us now?'

'Goodness no, no. They treated me to a tasty meal, and they gave me a cigar.'

The prisoners' joy was extraordinary. They passed from the waiting room of desperation to that of heaven.

'Thank God! Thank God!' groaned the priest. 'God has not forsaken us.'

The banker described the interview adding rather presumptuously,

'Besides, they have asked for my collaboration in the

new regime. It's something to think about. Because, after all, one is a specialist.'

When the prisoners learned that some food was being got ready, they impatiently paced one way and then the other. Peace of mind had awakened their appetites. Despite everything they felt that 'those communists were good boys.'

A box of cookies, milk and a bottle of white wine finally arrived. The food which had been evenly distributed among the prisoners by Don Nicanor, was gone within a few minutes.

The most pathetic scenes took place among the fugitives; those that had to flee from their dynamited, burned, and devastated homes. Whole families, carrying small suitcases containing their most indispensable items, began the exodus from the city in search of refuge. As it was extremely dangerous to cross the streets, these transient households passed through patios and yards with their burden of children and belongings. At times, it was necessary to break through the wall of a house to pass through from one to the other. There were families who had gone through seven party walls, driven by fires and sniping. Tenants opened life-saving breaches with axes, knives, hammers, and kitchen hooks. Sometimes they opened the road to the sepulcher, as there were those who on fleeing fell victim to ever-increasing street battles.

On those dull mornings, in doorways of homes well removed from the fighting, it was not unusual to find the families of a public servant, an artisan, or a clerk shivering from hunger and cold; having no idea what to do after spending an awful night full of explosions, illuminated by nearby fires.

One of these families had to evacuate their home with a sick old lady. They carried her in an armchair in the rain, without knowing where they were going. Some Red guards who came across the strange group led them all to the hospital. But the impression the old lady got when she entered the lobby filled with the wounded was such that she died before being placed in a bed. When the duty doctor came to deal with her, he said:

'You've brought nothing more than a corpse here!'

Other times the revolutionaries came across lost, horror-stricken men in doorways, whom they quickly asked,

'What are you doing here?'

'They've burned down my house and I don't know where to go.'

'But whose side are you on? With the Government or with the Revolution?'

'Well... I, look... I'm with you.'

'Well then, get a rifle, come on!'

They pushed him towards the firing line, and if the man did not manage to escape before reaching their headquarters, he would have to pick up a weapon and fight for Marxism.

Suárez, the magistrate, had hidden in a house close to his own, in company with his wife. It was midmorning, when they were all reciting the rosary, that a squad of revolutionaries arrived to the accompaniment of loud shouting and the clatter of rifle butts.

'Let's see! Who lives in this house?'

All the residents were giving their names. When it came to the magistrate's turn, a revolutionary pointed him out,

'This one's a fascist.'

The trembling magistrate said,

'No, no, I'm not a fascist.'

'He was involved in the August business,' shouted another.[39]

Suddenly, one of the revolutionaries fired his pistol at him,

'That will put a stop to your lying.'

The crazed magistrate's wife flung herself down to embrace her husband who had collapsed. She was hit in the arm by the second shot from his attacker who then calmly left carrying his weapon. Only the bleeding woman's cries of anguish and pain could be heard in the room. The other terrified residents were cringing in a corner. It was only after the revolutionary squad had left, taking the wounded woman to hospital, that they dared approach the corpse.

39 This is probably a reference to the 'Straperlo Affair' in which Alejandro Lerroux and Salazar Alonso accepted bribes from Daniel Strauss in order to legalize the fixed roulette. The ensuing scandal led to the fall of the Republican government, the arrival in power of the Popular Front and the radicalization of the Spanish parliament that led to the Spanish Civil War.

X – In The Towns

The Fishermen of Cimadevilla - The Death of the Leader - The Mayor and the Priest.

That the movement was a miners' uprising, scarcely controlled by workers' organizations, was borne out by the weak impact it had in the other towns of Asturias, including Gijón and Avilés. In Gijón, encouraged by the old anarchist José María Martínez, the fishermen of Cimadevilla and the workers of El Llano revolted. Cimadevilla is a neighborhood in old Gijón, squeezed onto a headland overlooking the dock. Those people who form a social group apart, hate spoiled young gentlemen. Consequently, men in cotton coveralls and sea boots, and brazen, saucy, chattering women carrying fish baskets, cause people strolling along Calle Corrida, to timidly move aside to let them pass. Revolutionary ferment is always present in Cimadevilla.

But in October they had scarcely any weapons. They vainly fought in the Plaza del Ayuntamiento. When the cruiser 'Libertad' stood off their neighborhood and fired its first salvo, the fishermen fled inland towards the workers' districts with their wives and children.

The largest contingent of the industrial workforce is to be found in El Llano and La Calzada. Those proletarians have endured heroic strikes and where necessary have not shirked violent measures. In Gijón, Spanish trade unionism has engaged in extremely bitter battles, even though rebelliousness has always predominated over organized struggle. This time, despite the efforts of José María Martínez, the trades unionists of Gijón stayed out of the *Alianza Obrera*. Those anarchists had not forgotten the differences which had always separated them from socialism; it intensified with the Republic. Consequently, the Gijón October was a weak popular outburst, from which the most violent sector of the proletariat was absent, that is those who follow the utopia of libertarian communism but are incapable of being part of a revolutionary doctrine. There was a time when the innate rebelliousness of the masses and the attraction of class warfare would have taken hold of the strikers. But the truth is that they lacked sufficient weapons and besides, the crew of the warship had disembarked without corroborating the rumors of rebellion.

Government forces easily dominated Cimadevilla, and without suffering major casualties, defeated the small group of revolutionaries who fought in El Llano. Several workers were killed in isolated engagements. Martínez, the leader, who had had violent arguments with the committees, was found dead on the road days later with a rifle by his side.

In Avilés, the workers captured the *Guardia Civil* positions, took the *Ayuntamiento* and fought in cooperation with the revolutionaries from Trubia. Pedregal, the *Partido Reformista* militant, was taken to Trubia and locked up in a tavern; the only attack he suffered was a slight bout of phlebitis. The same groups from Avilés dynamited a boat in San Juan de Nieva, to deny entrance to possible sea-borne forces.

In the rural towns in general, the revolution had scarcely any effect. There was hard fighting in Llanera. But in Grado and Salas where the local socialists had taken charge and carried out some requisitioning, it was little more than a revolutionary drill. The local committees deemed it necessary to detain the priest and the local *cacique*, enter the vestibule of the *Ayuntamiento* and order the closure of businesses. They then seized a radio to keep abreast of events, and a car to take the committee to Oviedo.

It was almost the same scene in all these towns. As the *guardias* had concentrated in the capital, the only civil forces left were the *guardias municipales*. An unruly group called at the mayor's house,

'Is Don Arturo in?'

His trembling wife came out,

'Well... he isn't in. He left very early.'

Then one of the militants, the one with the strongest personality, insisted,

'Right, right. Tell him to come out, we're not going to eat anyone here...'

The mayor, who moreover, was often politically left leaning, appeared friendlier than usual,

'But what's happening? My wife is scared and didn't want me to come out.'

'Look Don Arturo... You must already know that we're taking part in a revolution.'

'Yes. I've heard it said in Oviedo... Officially I don't know anything. Alright?'

'Well here...As you can see...We don't have any alternative. We are complying with the orders of the committee. You've got to hand the mayoralty over to us ...'

'Come on ... This thing about handing over...You could fail and then, what happens? A mayor has to be careful what he does.'

'Well, we need the *Ayuntamiento*.'

'Right; that's a different matter. You go there, and I won't make an appearance... Then it won't implicate anyone.'

They flocked to the *Ayuntamiento* and set up there for a time. But as they had to do something revolutionary, a group marched to the priest's house, he had just finished saying mass and talking to the early-rising little old ladies. The parish priest already knew the rebels. They were the town's awkward characters, the atheists, and the 'socialists.' The priest, wearing his grimy hat was somewhat disturbed to receive them.[40]

'But what's going on boys?'

'The revolution's broken out Don Federo.'

'Fine, fine. And what do you want from me?'

'Well, you know that we've taken over the *Ayuntamiento* and control the town. We want you to close the church.'

40 The strong anticlericalism of the Spanish Second Republic was driven by the Anarchists, Communists, and Socialists, as well as some of the Republicans despite the presence in the government of centrist Catholic Republicans like its first President, Niceto Alcalá Zamora, and Miguel Maura, Minister of the Interior. The approval of the 1931 Constitution that declared Spain a lay state as well as a series of measures designed to curtail the power of the Spanish Catholic Church triggered the resignation of Alcalá Zamora and Maura. The confrontation of the Spanish Second Republic would eventually become one of the main reasons for its implosion as the Republicans miscalculated the *de facto* power that the Church had. While fighting to retain its position of privilege, certain sectors of the Catholic Church sought to work to improve the situation of the working class. Father Maximiliano Arboleya, canon of the cathedral of Oviedo, was one of the leaders of what was known as *Catolicismo Social*. This branch of Catholicism advocated for social justice while rejecting what they perceived as the corrupting influence of everyday politics. In 1913, Arboleya founded the Casa del Pueblo Católica (Catholic House of the People) and the Síndicatos Independientes (Independent Trade Unions). Arboleya endured the criticism and, on occasion, condemnation from Rome of his activities to promote social justice. According to Julián Casanova, despite the efforts of Arboleya and other representatives of *Catolicismo Social*, it never managed to gain significant support from the workers that perceived the Catholic Church as a stout ally of the bosses (108-9).

'Why? It won't do the revolution any harm...'

The town's Marxist broke in,

'You'll find out that this is a revolution like in Russia. 'Religion is the opium of the people'.'

'My God, how the newspapers cloud your judgment! Religion is necessary.'

'For you lot,' one of the group insolently retorted.

'Fine, fine. I don't want to argue.'

'You must come with us to the *Ayuntamiento*.'

'Am I a prisoner?'

'No, come on, it's nothing to do with being a prisoner Don Federo... The committee will be there.'

The priest was led to the *Ayuntamiento* where he stayed until the evening when they authorized his return to the rectory. Meanwhile, the groups armed themselves with shotguns and pistols and patrolled the deserted streets.

The townspeople had gathered in the square and were discussing the news from the capital, and above all, that concerning local events which were of much greater importance there than the battles which were taking place at that time in Oviedo and Campomanes.

It was on the third day of the revolt when news arrived that La Vega Factory had been taken. It was a great revolutionary victory, and in some towns, they wanted to attack the stores and the owners' homes. The committees were very committed to calming the groups and even arranged some requisitioning of supplies with notes previously signed by the local committee to serve as a guarantee for the traders. Some clothing and foodstuffs were enough to pacify even the most hot-headed.

When it became known that military forces had entered Oviedo and that the revolution was failing, the panic among the revolutionaries in some towns was extraordinary. They dumped all their weapons into the river and the most compromised fled. At the same time, the so-called decent people appeared on the streets again; during the recent events, they had remained in their homes fearing local reprisals. The respectable gentlemen at the Casino, fearfully in hiding for a week, returned to their armchairs, insulting their neighbors and weaving the threads of betrayal and vengeance.

XI – The Committees Flee

Peña Withdraws - Clandestine Radio - The Communist Committee - In the Marquise's Villa - Teodomiro Menéndez, against the Reds.

The desertion of the first committee to operate in Oviedo took place on the twelfth day. Peña[41] knew of the defeat of the revolution in the rest of Spain and considered it prudent, due to aerial bombing, to withdraw the force which was fighting in disadvantageous conditions.

These arguments weighed on the minds of the leadership, almost all of them friends of Peña. But they did not dare raise the question on the floor of the Committee where there were major disagreements with the communists. The first internal conflict came about when the communists from Turón, on instructions from a member of the Miere's committee there, proclaimed the *República Obrera y Campesina de Asturias* during a clandestine radio broadcast. Through that action, the socialists saw that the communists were intent upon taking over the movement.

In reality no one dared slow the impetus of that armed mass which had been led to believe that the revolution constituted the end of their pain and misery. The truth is that

---

41 Ramón González Peña was the leader of the *Síndicato de Obreros Asturianos* (Asturian Workers Trade Union) during the Asturian revolution. He went on to become the president of the Socialist *Unión General de Trabajadores* (U.G.T.), a Member of Parliament, and Minister of Justice between 1938 and 1939.

the enthusiasm of some fighters was already beginning to wane. They had been surprised by the resistance of government forces, and above all, intimidated by the action of the airplanes, against which the revolutionaries lacked the means to combat, or resist.

In the final conversation that Peña had with his friends from Mieres, he declared that he was abandoning the fight. This is how it happened.

He and some friends organized a car and fled Oviedo. That same day López Ochoa's column entered the capital.[42] The socialist members of the committee, faced with this decision by the most representative figure of the movement, also fled. Only one communist remained, he immediately decided to convene a meeting of the leaders of all the groups. These, in the majority communist, were furious at the flight of the leadership and decided to carry on the struggle.

'We'll fight to the death!' they shouted.

'The revolution has been betrayed!'

'Let's find 'em and shoot 'em!'

A second committee, made up entirely of communists, was immediately constituted. Five young men and two older workers decided to go on fighting. This committee transferred to a luxurious villa belonging to the Marqués de Aledo in Plazuela San Miguel; it had been occupied by the revolutionaries from the very beginning. For the first time, the rich carpets of Herrero's villa were trodden by miners' boots as they trailed in lumps of bloodied mud.

42 Eduardo López Ochoa, Spanish general that led the military repression of the Asturias revolt. López Ochoa was demonized in many of the revolutionist pamphlets published after the 1934 revolution. The pamphlet *Los crímenes de la reacción española* produced by the *Spanish section of the Comintern agency International Red Aid (SRI)*, accused López Ochoa of encouraging his soldiers to commit all kinds of cruelties against the miners as well as stealing the contents of the safe in the Bank of Asturias. (Bunk 2002: 74)

The hall was full of rifles and boxes of ammunition. The fighters' weapons and clothing were jumbled up on tables and armchairs. Piles of proclamations were spread about the floor and even out onto the sandy courtyard. A constant coming and going of men asking for weapons, of women looking for food coupons, lent the villa the air of a temporary encampment.

The first thing the committee did was to agree that Teodomiro Menéndez, the most important socialist, be ordered to appear.[43] At that time, workers had become so agitated, that many were discussing shooting him. One communist opposed it,

'Teodomiro has never been with the revolution. But he hasn't deceived anyone. He can't be blamed for the faults of others.' The point of view prevailed that he should be summoned to make him aware of the flight of his comrades. The committee charged two armed workers to find him.

'If he doesn't want to come, bring him to me by force,' said the chairman.

Half an hour later, Teodomiro appeared between the Red guards. When he was in front of the new committee, looking somewhat pallid, and agitated, he protested,

'You sent armed men to look for me, like an enemy. I can't understand this treatment comrades.'

A great commotion broke out among the committee members,

'Aren't you aware that all your comrades have escaped? You've all betrayed the revolution.'

43 Teodomiro Menéndez was a socialist syndicalist leader that participated actively in the Asturias revolt despite not being in in favor of it. After the defeat of the revolutionaries, he was jailed and eventually released when the Popular Front gained power in 1936.

'You've tricked us,' bellowed another.

'The revolution isn't defeated,' shouted the one who seemed more composed than the rest.

Teodomiro Menéndez replied,

'Tell me when I may speak.'

'Speak', said the person acting as chairman. 'But be aware they'll demand someone's head for this.'

Teodomiro began by saying, 'It seems impossible that someone who has spent around forty years as a militant, defending the workers, should receive such unjust treatment. I'm experiencing the greatest distress of my life. I don't know if you're aware that my wife is gravely ill, and that the disasters of the recent days have added to the terrible pain of seeing how my companion might die at any moment. Comrades, you know full well that I've been opposed to the revolution; I believed it was doomed from the very first day...'[44]

'You're wrong,' interrupted someone not on the committee.

'This is cowards' talk,' muttered another.

'Quiet!' shouted the chairman. 'He needs to be heard. The comrade is speaking honestly. What we wouldn't stand for is lying.'

Teodomiro went on to say, 'Comrades, you must understand that because I didn't want to deceive anyone I didn't join in. I believe that, given the forces available to the Government, unless the whole of Spain rises, no triumph is possible.'

---

44 As a Socialist leader, Teodomiro Menéndez's words here are especially poignant. Teodomiro lived through the bloody repression of the 1917 general strike, and unlike other syndicalists, refused to collaborate with the dictator Primo de Rivera when he offered to negotiate with the miners in 1923 shortly after taking power. As a staunch defender of Indalecio Prieto's position within the Socialist party, Teodomiro represented a call for a more engaged reformism.

'Madrid has risen', said one.

'It isn't certain. Sadly, the radio news is genuine. In Barcelona, the *Generalitat* has surrendered and in Madrid there was nothing more than sporadic shooting. We can't delude ourselves. The revolution is defeated. To prolong the struggle is to increase the catastrophe.'

'Comrade,' declared the chairmen, 'we have not summoned you to lecture us. The struggle continues because the workers want to go on. We have to tell you that because of the flight of your socialist comrades who made up part of the committee, another which is taking responsibility for the movement has been constituted. I'm telling you this so that everyone remains at his post.'

'Right. I understand. But permit me to say to you that in my opinion, my comrades had no alternative.'

'They're traitors!', someone shouted.

The chairman went on, 'And besides, their arrest has been ordered. They must answer to the revolutionary tribunal for their flight.'

'In the name of our ideals will you not allow me to insist on what I believe is my duty?'

'No comrade. We are determined to go on...'

At that moment, a revolutionist came into the room bawling out,

'A column has entered Rubín Barracks. It came by the Avilés road.'

Everyone leapt up. Amid terrific confusion, men without weapons grabbed hold of them,

'Well, let's die fighting,' said one.

'We'll attack with dynamite! Call the people from Turón to come to us!' ordered the chairman of the committee.

They were no longer taking any notice of Teodomiro, He asked the chairman, 'Can I go back home!'

'You can go back. The password is now 'T.R.S.' (Red Workers, Greetings). I'm telling you in case you are stopped.'

While the revolutionaries were loudly arguing to the clatter of weapons and furniture, punctuated by swearing and threats. Teodomiro Menéndez, for many years a leader of the Asturian workers, returned home broken and sad. He was doubtlessly thinking all was lost; that dreams spread over so many noble and enthusiastic campaigns had only produced a harvest of disappointment and blood. He had not fled; in his humanitarian and sentimentalist heart his affection held sway over the interests of the revolution. He realized then that his work was finished, and it did not matter to him that his power over the masses had ended. His was the failure of a socialism which wanted to change the world by words, a fragile tool in a violent environment. He who over many years had wanted the salvation of the pariahs, at that moment, while explosions thundered, and bullets whistled from crazed machine guns, he asked only for the salvation of his life companion, of that simple, hard-working woman who was now bedridden with labored breath, and eyes half-closed by fever.

XII – Difficult Times

López Ochoa's Entry - Scenes at Puerta Nueva – Flight of the Second Committee - The Mark of Nero.

From that moment chaos and confusion reigned in the revolutionary camp despite the unequivocal orders of the new committee, and the bravery still shown by many of the revolutionaries.

López Ochoa and his column had unexpectedly appeared along the coast road, retaking some *Guardia Civil* positions which had been besieged for many days, and easily putting down the revolutionaries from Salas to Lugones. When the troops appeared at Rubín Barracks, its defenders opened fire believing they were the enemy. Once inside the barracks, the general planned the recapture of Oviedo. But it did not mean that the city would immediately be under his control. There was fighting, but it was only when troops from the Legion and *Regulares* arrived, that the revolutionaries were repulsed and forced to withdraw to the mining towns.

The second committee presided over nothing but anarchy and reprisals. Looting and indiscipline worsened with the news of the entry of the troops. Patrols which had reached the brothels at Puerta Nueva, remained there. Women trembled and crowded together in the kitchens, but the miners took them out and made them dance, cheering them on, beating out the rhythm with their rifle butts. They brought crates of wine and beer from a nearby tavern, and that saddest of nights, despite the din of gunfire, drunken singing could be heard in the ruins of Oviedo. The young women sitting on the miners' knees were afraid and hungry, trembling not with passion but with panic. One of them was from Langreo, and she was anxiously asking about her brothers, who had clearly been fighting from the very first day. But nobody knew anything about them. A miner consoled her,

'Don't worry honey. If they're in hospital, there's no shooting there and if they died, all the better for them.'

Some of them danced with rifles over their shoulders, and cartridge belts around their waists, taken from dead *guardias*.

They needed to forget; after a week's fighting, breathing powder and blood, with the premonition of imminent defeat, they had entered the dead-end of a strange despair. Everything they said was loaded with sarcasm, they drank without rhyme or reason, wetted their hands which were burning from handling their overheated weapons. Candlelight cast living shadows onto the walls; that strained, gloomy binge was the saddest part of the revolution. They all drank in such a way that by dawn they were sick or unconscious. Overpowered by tiredness, they began to collapse, one here and another there, on the staircase, in the dining room, in the other rooms of the houses. The horrible, murky, ashen dawn found those piled up bogus corpses; they lay there many hours while in the streets other fighters fell never to rise again.

Some of the members of the first committee were captured on the same day as their flight. The second committee discussed the penalty they had incurred. One proposed shooting them. In the end, they imposed the kindest judgment and pardoned them, as such they were to take up a weapon and fight. The former committeemen, fought in the vanguard under command of the squad leaders, against the troops of General López Ochoa.

No one obeyed the second committee. The revolutionaries acted on their own authority, and whatever initiative, however recklessly extreme it might be, was well received by the groups. It could be said that the period of terror had begun, because even though dynamite had been used from the start, it always met certain battlefield requirements. Now it was used without any concrete objective, for the simple desire to destroy. The revolution had gone mad and it was dizzily plunging into chaos.

What was going to happen? Ramón Tol, the doctor our readers already know of who alternated between treating the wounded and taking an active part in the fighting, gradually became aware that the idea of destroying the city was taking hold among the fighters. As they could no longer win, and as government forces were advancing on Oviedo, they would find only ruins. That Nero-like idea was not held by anyone in particular, but it was already widespread among the revolutionaries. The doctor, appalled by such a proposition, went to the house where the committee sat and set out his fears. In fact, he met with a dithering, nervy group, who seemed so unlike the previous day's men, who had so bravely taken control of the movement.

Ramón Tol said, 'I believe that you should get the group leaders together and order them not to tolerate any discussion of it whatsoever.'

'But they don't take any notice! They're acting of their own accord. The movement's slipping from our hands,' admitted the worried chairman.

'Steps must be taken', replied the doctor, If they carry out what they say, not only would it be an act of stupidity it would also discredit our revolution.'

'You're right comrade. But are you sure they're talking about it?'

'Absolutely. I've heard several in less than an hour.'

'We need to speak to the group leaders. There's no alternative.'

'We've called them, but they haven't turned up,' said another committee member.

A third said, 'Look, it's best to leave them to it, they understand one another.'

Ramón Tol believed the proposition would raise an uproar of protests; but he was surprised to see that the others kept quiet, as though they were mulling it over, or had previously agreed to it. Fear and disappointment had seized the second committee too. It patently lacked authority, initiative, and energy. Tol then demanded the chairman accompany him to speak to some of the group leaders. Along the way, the chairman complained to the doctor,

'This was headless at birth comrade. I don't know how we're going to get out of it. I get the feeling that Teodomiro was right; they have left us on our own, apart from here nobody is fighting.'

'Then I propose a withdrawal,' said Tol, convinced he was right.

'And who would dare to propose such a thing? They would say we'd sold out. The other day a squad leader held a pistol against my chest because I told him I would not tolerate looting.'

'Then it's a problem that needs to be raised.'

The doctor and the chairman headed for the Northern Station where the revolutionaries' advanced positions were.

They spoke to a few group leaders who scarcely gave the subject any importance. One said reassuringly,

'We will still win comrades. There's no need to worry. The troops got into the barracks and are scared to come out.'

'But to blow up Oviedo would be an outrage,' said the doctor.

'If we can't have it comrade, then no one else can.'

They went to San Lorenzo where the gun was emplaced; no one there wanted to hear anything about committees or about union officials,

'I think the committees have escaped. Alright, well, we're not leaving this. What brave, good-for-nothing, union officials!'

The two revolutionaries withdrew convinced that there was no way to control the rampaging masses. The chairman of the committee declared that he was stepping down from his post. When they arrived at Villa Herrero, the rest were no longer there. The second committee had also disappeared.

Ramón Tol realized it was essential to avoid a catastrophe at all costs. During his trip to Langreo he had been able to confirm that there was a plucky leader there, who had great influence among all the important workers. This leader, Belarmino Tomás, might perhaps at that moment take the reins of the movement. The doctor looked for a Red Cross car and asked to be taken to Sama on urgent business. The head of the hospital authorized the journey, but it was through gritted teeth.

In Sama, Tol found Belarmino at the *Ayuntamiento* busy with supplying Langreo valley. Belarmino Tomás with his beret, calm expression, and intelligent gaze, was surrounded by people asking for coupons; it took quite a long time before he had time for the doctor.[45] They finally talked at length. Belarmino was aware of the situation in Oviedo and knew that troops were advancing from Gijón and San Esteban de Pravia. It was urgent of course, to organize the withdrawal,

'But this is the most difficult part', said Belarmino. After all, a revolution is a war and in war the most difficult thing is the withdrawal.'

'Besides, said Tol, 'there are those who if they have weapons will not withdraw.'

'No one will convince them that it has failed completely in the rest of Spain.'

'But what is deadly serious is that they're talking of blowing up the city.'

'Is that what they're saying?' Said Belarmino in alarm.

'They go on about it too much.'

'Oh! Something must be done. I'll go to Oviedo with you right now.'

On the way, they met only workers returning to their homes with rifles on their shoulders. The sentries who had previously demanded car passes, had disappeared. It all had an air of desolation, of disillusionment and of defeat.

Belarmino said,

---

45 Belarmino Tomás, leader of the Asturian Miners Trade Union (SOMA) and member of the Miners Federation in the socialist trade union (UGT), was one of the syndicalist to publicly ask the revolutionaries to abandon the revolt. "This," Belarmino explained, "does not mean that we abandon the class struggle. Our surrender today will not be more than a temporary stop that will allow us to correct our mistakes and prepare ourselves for our next battle" (qtd. in Peirats, 85).

'We lacked leadership. Besides, you can't fight against airplanes. At the very least, you need equivalent weaponry.'

No one asked for their passes on entering Oviedo, nor the password. However, they could hear gun and rifle fire. That afternoon airplanes again flew over the barracks and dropped supplies. The revolutionaries fired at them, but it was useless.

Belarmino held meetings with several of the most important fighters and that night convened a meeting in Villa Herrero, already there was no trace of the second committee, save for empty bottles and countless cigarettes. Most of the group leaders and many important socialists and communists attended. They acknowledged that it was essential to transfer the leadership of the movement out of Oviedo. Should the troops marching on the capital succeed in taking it, there was still the mining valley, where the Reds considered themselves invincible. Knowing every inch of the terrain and supplied by their families, the struggle could go on indefinitely in the almost inaccessible mountains, and Asturias would continue to be the bulwark of the proletarian revolution. This was the idea of the most admired fighters. They had failed to realize that depression had already taken hold of the masses, and that the ardent hopes of the first days were absent. It was impossible to rebuild the belief in triumph and the generating spirit of victory that Peña's withdrawal had undone. Belarmino and the doctor perfectly understood that all was lost; but they also understood that it would only be possible by means of an indirect, roundabout route, to reach the terrible conclusion that they had to capitulate. Consequently, they agreed to everything, even managing to inject a little order into the chaos, putting a brake on the desperate reaction of the masses.

After planning next day's renewed attack on the prison, the headquarters and the *Gobierno Civil*, the new committee set out in the Red Cross car for Sama de Langreo. It was the first step toward capitulation.

XIII – Capitulation

The Final Assaults - Lacking Munitions - The Third Committee decides on Withdrawal - The Meeting with the General

On the sixteenth day, enemy positions were resolutely attacked. It was above all about capturing the prison which held important revolutionaries whose presence would undoubtedly influence the fighters' spirits. It was not possible. The garrison held out by twice repulsing besiegers with the bayonet.

As night fell, they requested more munitions. But headquarters replied they were needed to attack the barracks from where troops were attempting to come to their aid. The attack on the prison had to be suspended, as had the attack on the *Gobierno Civil*, it was still being defended from the Cathedral. As their cartridge pouches were empty, the revolutionaries asked one another for ammunition.

They asked the group leaders, 'Are there any more rounds left?'

'No. They've sent for some at Sama. But today we've got to manage with the ammo boxes they delivered this morning.'

That was demoralizing. Bored-looking miners could be seen, leaning against doorways, with their rifles thrown on the ground,

'Aren't you fighting son?'

'What with? I don't have a bullet left.'

'Son; this is really bad...'

'The leadership has abandoned us...'

They had completely wasted munitions. The revolution had lacked a technical- military concept from the very start. It had been entrusted solely to the personal courage of the workers, who failed to recognize the value of munitions. The capture of La Vega Factory had deluded them into believing that those munitions would never run out, that the mutinous warships would arrive at any moment with reinforcements, that Russia would send its fleet as far as the Cantabrian coast to aid the epic struggle of the Asturian mountain dwellers. Simple, excited souls - the most absurd rumors were enough to stoke up the fires of belief in and fervor for the struggle. They thought that a mysterious power was working almost miraculously during those days. They believed that the momentum which led them to die for their ideals would have sufficient force to carry over onto all the actions of the revolution. In a word, they trusted in the power and strength of their class, fired up by their propagandists in speeches and proclamations.

Not until the committee received the request for munitions, did it realize they had run out. Consequently, some reinforcements were organized in Mieres. The troops there had been able to break the siege of Vega de Rey, and in the ensuing panic, were advancing on towns and villages. The committee which was meeting in the *Ayuntamiento* at Langreo received pessimistic news from all the areas. Finally, Belarmino Tomás tabled the question,

'Comrades, the situation is untenable. We have fought to the last. There's nothing to do but capitulate.'

The committee still held out. It needed to personally consider the situation in Oviedo, examine the morale of the fighters and gain an exact appreciation of the state of the troops. Next day the different members of the committee left for Oviedo and Mieres on a reconnoitring mission. Impressions could not have been more distressing. In Mieres fighting had broken out between the workers themselves, and there were mounting fears of internal conflict. In Oviedo, the demoralization reached alarming levels. Quarrels and ructions increased. There were mass desertions now without pretexts or excuses. Attacks on stores, coupled with drunkenness and arguments were increasing in frequency. Guard duty was not regularly performed, and liaison hardly functioned. If the forces in the Rubín Barracks had come out at any time, they would easily have taken the city; days before it would have been inaccessible to an entire army corps. Munitions were on the point of running out, and only artillery and dynamite, occasionally demonstrated that the revolution had not yet lost its voice. In the streets, nothing could be seen other than people collecting the remains of booty, carrying off all kinds of objects, searching through the rubble, and robbing corpses. It was plain to see that it was not those who had fought, rather those who had emerged from their hiding places to take advantage of the pause in the revolution.

The impact on the members of the committee could hardly have been worse. On the morning of the seventeenth day, the third revolutionary committee convened in the *Ayuntamiento* at Sama. The rumor was circulating that the struggle was going to be called off, and a crowd made up of workers and the families of fighters began to gather in the square. While the committee was deliberating, down below impassioned arguments were raging on what the day's outcome would bring. Very few maintained the need to carry on resisting. Although the majority would deny confessing to it, deep down everyone wished for an armistice. Everyone had been tortured by the horrors of those ten days, and all to a greater or lesser extent, carried its mark imprinted on their heart.

It was a fraught committee meeting. Everyone agreed on the need to capitulate, but where they disagreed was over the conditions of the surrender. There were even some who expected General López Ochoa to grant them prior recognition, as the emissaries were in effect from the Red Army. If the Turón broadcast had announced the proclamation of the so-called Workers and Peasants Republic of Asturias, it followed that there existed an army with which to negotiate.

Finally, an agreement was reached. To expedite the cessation of hostilities, a proposal would be made to the commanding general that troops should not enter the mining area tactically, and that no colonial forces should figure in the vanguard.[46] For their part the revolutionaries agreed to call off the struggle and abandon the capital and the coalfields.

Belarmino Tomás went out onto the balcony and gave the waiting crowd an account of the agreement. He spoke with simplicity and feeling of the revolutionaries' efforts, of the inferior conditions in which they found themselves, of the spilled blood and devastated homes. 'We go on believing', he said, 'that it is our right and we have not resigned ourselves to losing it.' He ended by asking the impromptu assembly,

---

46 Despite their importance in the repression of the Asturias revolution, Díaz Fernández makes scarce mention to Francisco Franco's colonial troops. In fact, unlike López Ochoa, Francisco Franco is never mentioned.

'Do you approve of the committee's proposal?'

A unanimous cry, partly choked by emotion, answered,

'Yes.'

They wanted peace, not through conviction, not through regret, rather through weariness, through physical exhaustion, through the wish to rest free from the terrible shock of the struggle. It had been so long since they had eaten in peace, since food had been rationed, since machine guns had been hammering, sowing shock throughout the valley! Finally, the dreadful bomb-carrying birds would stop appearing over the peaks. It would soon be possible to walk freely along the streets without having to check every step for sounds from above of the sinister flight of the enemy carrying fire and death in its talons.

Belarmino Tomás, together with a prisoner of the revolutionaries, Lieutenant Torrens of the *Guardia Civil*, were charged with transmitting the proposal to General López Ochoa. Apparently, Torrens knew the general and would testify that the emissary represented the revolutionary committee.

The negotiators arrived at Rubín Barracks with their hands up. In fact, the sentries immediately took them prisoner. When the general was apprised of the reason for their mission, he allowed them in. Belarmino Tomás began by observing that the workers were negotiating with an acknowledged republican general, and then gave him an account of the terms of surrender. The general made his own proposals, the surrender of a quarter of the revolutionary committee; the hand-over of weapons and the complete cessation of hostilities.

The agreement was signed at midday. The committee circulated the orders for withdrawal which were complied with, but not without some difficulties. The intention of the leaders was to abandon Oviedo that same night, as the colonial troops were already breathing down their necks.

XIV – The Evacuation Of Oviedo

Difficulties – The Wayward Gun – Silence in the Ruins - The Institute is Blown Up

That strange encampment, which for eleven days had been Oviedo, was going to be struck within a few hours. Man puts down roots everywhere, even in war, even in misery, in prison and in hospital. Despite the hardship of those disastrous days, despite constant danger, of fatigue and want, many men took a liking to the revolution. To return to the harshness of the mine, to the monotonous, everyday drudgery, after having dreamt of a new existence, breaking the chains of manual work, was a bitter pill. When the delegates from the committee arrived with the message to call off the struggle and withdraw towards Langreo, they were met with a great deal of negativity.

'We'll fight to the death!' they said.

'When we're out of bullets, we'll fight with knives.'

In some positions the revolutionaries were lying down not taking any notice of the orders they had received. Furious or downcast, the miners kept on refusing to abandon the capital. And those who did, roundly refused to deliver up their weapons.

Belarmino Tomás had to go around all the positions together with communist leaders to make sure the order was obeyed. Grudgingly, the most unwilling miners took their places in vans and trucks, protesting,

'We could have saved ourselves from a huge disaster.'

The most stubborn said, 'They've tricked us', .'

But once in the vehicle, they were happy that the nightmare had ended, and were finally looking forward to getting home for a sound sleep, free from the snatched naps taken during those tragic days.

However, the gun at San Lázaro went on thundering. They had sent those combatants messages to cease fire, despite firing being futile as the shells had no timers. Belarmino was extremely angry because that gun seemed to prove that the workers were not adhering to the agreement. He decided to go and deal with it himself, along with a group of stalwarts.

The gun was served by a gunner from Trubia who was firing under orders from a group from Mieres. Belarmino spoke to the gunner,

'But haven't you already received orders to cease fire?'

'I'm under orders to go on firing.'

'Let's see, where's your group leader?'

The group leader, a thickset youth with an unbuttoned shirt and hostile look, appeared in the doorway of a nearby house. He carried a pistol and was followed by half a dozen armed men.

Belarmino addressed him,

'Don't you recognize me comrade?'

The youth looked at him somewhat darkly. Then he spoke,

'Yes. I know you're Belarmino, from Sama.

'Why haven't you ceased firing? The committee has agreed it.'

'I don't know about committees,' answered the angry miner. 'Some say the committees have run away; others that they're negotiating with the troops. I don't know anything. Peña was the one who nominated me for this, and he hasn't yet told me to stop'.

'We won't surrender,' interjected another of the armed youths. 'If they want the gun, let them come for it.'

Belarmino calmly talked to them about the conditions on which the surrender had been agreed. The struggle was lost, and it was essential to avoid reprisals in homes in the coalfields. The socialist ideal had not been defeated and they would have the chance to fight for it again. But all the difficulties they raised then would only prejudice the workers' cause.

The leader's words struck home and the revolutionaries gave way,

'But we're not going to hand over our weapons. Never'

Belarmino told them to get into a van back to Mieres. The miners resignedly set out on the journey towards the city center. The gun had finally been silenced, and there it remained like a dead beast alone in the middle of the street.

The miners trailed their weapons towards the vehicles. Some carried souvenirs of the struggle, *Guardia de Asalto* gaiters, a sabre, a service pistol. Others set out on foot, in no hurry to get there as they were hoping cars would pick them up on the way. Extreme weariness and limitless indifference was apparent in all of them. There was scarcely any talk among the groups. As the revolutionaries left, the city appeared ever more tragic, silent, and devastated. After many days of terrifying turmoil in which human voices meld with the noise of weaponry, that calm was perhaps even more anguished. In that bituminous night, the smoking embers of the fires, the timid footsteps of some passer-by, clogged corners, the houses bleeding from their flanks, all presented a dreadful, gory air. Oviedo was in effect, a petrified, motionless city, haemorrhaging in silence. Not even the airplanes had appeared that afternoon. The last of the trucks which had evacuated the city, stood with its engine loudly juddering, until it also died away, like the last echo of the struggle.

But suddenly an immense explosion like an earthquake shook that fleeting calm. It shook the city as though its roots had just been torn away, as though a mountain had fallen. What had happened? The Institute where the revolutionaries had stored their dynamite had blown up.

Hours before, the prisoners who were held there had been freed by order of the committee. No one knew who had said the building should be blown up. There certainly were about twenty boxes of dynamite there (close to five thousand cartridges) and various crates of bombs made at the factories at La Felguera and Mieres, some weighed up to thirty kilos.

Near midnight, four revolutionaries were checking that neighboring homes had been evacuated by their tenants. The latter were so panic-stricken that they did not even ask reason for that measure. They hastily fled toward the other side of the city. They were so accustomed to the horrors of the revolution that nothing touched them; the one thing they did was blindly obey the workers' instructions. An old man who had followed the course of the struggle with interest, and who already knew the revolutionaries from that sector, asked the reason for the move.

'We're going to get rid of our dynamite, so they don't get it.'

'Oh! You don't say,' the old man replied with conviction. 'Like Cervera in the Cuban War.'

'Did he also blow the dynamite?'

'They say it sank the boats.'

When no one was left in the neighborhood, those who had until then been on guard in the building, started moving away. However, in one of the classrooms that morning one of the sentries was in a deep, drunken sleep. He had been heavily drinking every day in the tavern across the road. His comrades said that this exemplary fighter had done nothing over the ten days of occupation in Oviedo but confiscate every type of drink and incessantly down it. He spent his days in a drunken stupor.

The revolutionaries wanted to wake him, but it was pointless. They shook him violently, called him again and again, but the drunkard went on snoring. Then one of the revolutionaries dragged him out of the room, but when he got to the stairs he turned to his comrades,

'Do you know what I'm going to say comrades? We ought to leave him here.'

'If we leave him, he sure won't drink again in this life.'

'A revolutionary who gets drunk instead of fighting doesn't deserve to be saved.'

'You're right. Let him drink in hell.'

And they left him there. The landing with the dynamite was doused with gasoline, they set it alight and ran, minutes later the explosion sowed panic in the city. Upon hearing it, terrified people came out of their homes, shouting and running in all directions.

What new catastrophe had that din brought the martyred city? What fresh horrors still awaited the overwhelmed neutral population who were frozen with fear and hunger, whose ears still rang with the terrifying uproar of war?

It took some time for the city to calm. When it became known that the revolutionaries had detonated their explosives, no one was sure whether other dumps existed and whether the feared explosions would continue.

Despite everything, calm did not return. Fighting went on in the outlying districts of Oviedo. In Naranco, groups of revolutionaries withstood the advanced guard of the Legion which arrived after tough days. It had been a disorderly evacuation, and besides, many fighters were still in possession of their rifles and machine guns. That was where '*La Libertaria*'[47] died. The young woman was the daughter of an anarchist who had dressed in red for the struggle. It seemed impossible that days of fighting had gone by without '*La Libertaria*' suffering injury; her red clothes offered the perfect target. She was there when the colonial forces entered, firing her rifle from behind a barricade, while other comrades also fired their rifles and machine guns.

The officer of the advanced guard could not believe it was a woman who was firing.

'I'd like to take her alive,' said the lieutenant.

But within a few moments a shot knocked her onto a roadside barrier. With the revolutionaries driven off, the soldiers stared at her, somewhat surprise by what they saw as incomprehensible heroism. '*La Libertaria*' lay there like a red pool in the middle of the road until the next day when an ambulance collected the corpse; it was buried in

---

47 María Silva Cruz (1915-1936) was a member of the CNT and an active participant in the 1933 demonstration in Casas Viejas that was violently repressed by the Spanish Civil Guard. As the workers escaped the Civil Guard, many took refuge in Cruz's family house. The Civil Guard set fire to the house burning Cruz's entire family alive. Cruz survived but was later assassinated at the onset of Franco's failed *coup d'état* that led to the Spanish Civil War. Spanish writer Ramón J. Sender chronicled the events of 1933 in his documentary novel *Viaje a la aldea del crimen* (1934).

a communal grave. She was twenty years old and a communist.

The city had been evacuated by the revolutionaries and the troops had taken over complete control. Strange, stunned, and incoherent beings began to appear on the streets. It was as though they had returned from a ghostly world after a nightmare existence. Women were crying without knowing why, men told of grotesque or tragic incidents, and went back to their boltholes, unconvinced that it had all come to an end.

People who did not know each other talked about the anguish of the revolution.

'And what's happening in Madrid? What's happening in Madrid?'

An agitated, bald man, in a stained and creased suit which appeared not to have been changed for many days, could do no more than badger everyone with that question. He also accosted an officer who was walking down Calle Fruela, asking,

'What's happening in Madrid?'

The officer gave him a scornful look and replied,

'Nothing's happening in Madrid. What's going to happen?'

Doubtless, the bald man had reason enough to ask that question. He had arrived in Oviedo on the eve of the revolution. He was a pharmacist in Madrid and had gone to the capital to deal with an important order for a German product which he represented in Spain. He lodged in the Hotel Inglés in Oviedo where from the start a group of *Guardia de Asalto* had set up with the intention of blocking the revolutionaries' path. On the sixth day, the guest was woken by an horrendous din, the sound of running and shouting, followed by the dry crack of rifle fire. Someone shouted to him that the revolution had broken out and the miners were attacking the hotel. He was forced to spend two days there without a mouthful of food, confined to rooms at the rear with other equally terrified guests. The miners finally took the building and detained all its occupants. The pharmacist was taken before the committee and subjected to a thorough grilling,

'What were you doing in the building comrade?'

I was a guest in the Hotel Inglés.'

'Where do you normally live?'

'In Madrid.'

'And what is your occupation?'

'Pharmacist.'

'Oh, a Pharmacist? We need pharmacists. Are you with the revolution?'

'Well, I...the truth is. I've never been involved in politics.'

'Right; you're a petty bourgeois without a party. You're going to take charge of a pharmacy in Escandalera. I take it that you won't poison our sick.'

'Good Lord! But...it would be better if someone else did it. I'm just so upset.'

'There's no alternative. You'll be better there than stopping a bullet when you least expect it.'

The pharmacist had no alternative but to take charge of the pharmacy and dispatch the coupons sent to him by the director of the hospital. Incidentally, he constantly received exorbitant requests for specialist equipment, and all kinds of medical supplies.

His industrialist spirit was infuriated by such wastefulness,

'Really', he would say to the messengers, 'tell them not to waste so much; they're going to end up without any stocks and then what's going to happen...'

During that time, he also thought about his beloved pharmacy in Madrid, would the same thing be happening, leaving him with an irreparable situation. For that man the tragedy lay principally in the over liberal use of medical stocks. Latterly, he reached the point where he took that problem so seriously that he could do nothing more than send notes to the committee regarding stocks, insisting that it used its influence to avoid those abuses.

Consequently, when the miners evacuated Oviedo and people came out onto the street after so many horrors, the pharmacist was obsessively inquiring what was happening in Madrid. To learn that his pharmacy was still intact would be the greatest satisfaction of his life.

XV – The Escape

Through the mountains - Ramón Tol's group – Night - The Defeated

Many miners returned to their homes. Others met up in Sama where the weapons had to be collected, although during the first days very few were handed in. But some groups fled through the mountains, prepared to put themselves beyond the reach of the troops, some because they had been in charge, others because the revolution had already placed them outside the law and into a life fraught with danger. The *Guardia Civil* were hunting down many of those groups who had carried on the fight for days. Others managed to scatter over the western mountains towards Galicia, and in some hamlets, others were captured without having time to fight back.

The group led by Doctor Ramón Tol, went on foot in a westerly direction because no van wanted to take them by the inland roads. Ramón Tol planned to go as far as his local parish, which was tucked away on the border with Galicia, and from there with an experienced guide, cross into Portugal on horseback. Another three young revolutionaries offered to go with him.

'But the first thing you must do', said the doctor, 'is leave your weapons behind.'

'And what are we going to defend ourselves with?'

'With pistols.'

'We don't have any.'

'See if you can find somebody who might trade your rifles.'

In the end, they managed the exchange. The four men set out without food or equipment of any sort. The doctor gave them instructions,

'Don't speak to the locals. Leave it to me, I know them well. The success of our escape depends on our being in La Espina by this time tomorrow.'

'Couldn't we find a car to take us there?' said one of the fugitives.

'I don't think it's probable or advisable. Besides, they could denounce us. The answer is to reach my village before the troops realize there could also be escapees over on this side.'

It was a difficult trek because the doctor did not want to follow the main road as he had pencil-traced a somewhat unusual itinerary. The mountains were flooded, the roads had turned into quagmires and the sky was scored with black, rain clouds, which threatened to pour onto the faded, bleak countryside.

The four men silently walked on. One of them suddenly whispered,

'This time we lost.'

'But next time we'll win,' said Ramón Tol, as though talking to himself. 'We lacked direction and unity. You can only fight with like weaponry. Today isn't like the seventeenth, when miners could build strongholds in the mountains and fight against the soldiers. There were no airplanes then. If only we had had airplanes...'

'That's what demoralized us most. Besides we didn't have leaders. Being brave isn't enough to lead a revolution.[48] A revolution has to be planned like a war.'

48 This is Díaz Fernández final subversion of the trope of masculine courage that informed most revolutionary pamphlets. Courage had been presented previously in the novel as an equalizer between revolutionaries and

They scarcely slept that night. Up at Salas one of them pointed out a village where they would be able to buy something in the tavern. He bought bread and sausage.

The doctor shared out the food equally, and then they lay down in a dry spot in the mountain undergrowth. Ramón Tol hardly slept, but for three or four hours his comrades were lost in a deep sleep. The doctor had to wake them to continue the journey.

There was a moon and it made their walk easier. At times the stars shone like lost objects in the pools in the road. The mass of the trees, enlarged by the shadows, seemed to loom over the fugitives. In a distant village, a dog barked, and another bark meld with the first, traveling in unison through the silence of the rural night.

They arrived at La Espina pass at dawn. There was a serene silence high up there on the solitary peaks. Dawn broke the last canvas of the autumnal night and the fields began to unveil their irregular shapes, their hues, and the smudge of their villages. The roosters broke the crystal air with their metallic cock-a-doodle-dos. For those fresh from the turmoil of the struggle, having heard the explosion of bombs, the thunder of artillery and dynamite, that peacefulness was something unexpected and new.

The revolutionaries were indifferent to the landscape. They were happy despite the tiring day's journey. They had gone a long way, and by midday would be in the village, from where the doctor knew escape would be easy. They entered Tineo parish. Ramón Tol imagined how that landscape must once have witnessed the passage of a much

---

armed forces. At the end of the novel, Díaz Fernández bluntly confronts the reader with the fact that courage alone may not be enough for political success.

more important revolutionary than themselves, Riego, the constitutional leader, hanged by the reactionaries. But Riego had not passed through there in flight, rather in triumph in his new sub-lieutenant's uniform. Besides, that liberalism was misguided. He believed that liberty merely had to be written down in various statute books for it to then exist. The doctor scorned that idea from the heights of his historic materialism. It seemed impossible to him that such people could be so naïve as to be unable to grasp that without economic liberty there is no spiritual liberty.

The doctor was accustomed to thinking in Marxist terms. Consequently, those thoughts assailed him despite his tiredness. Near midday their path was cut by the Narcea, a powerful river which runs on its long journey under silver birch, cherry, and chestnut trees. The doctor greeted it like an old friend. The river had been his companion in rides through the country. Tol was hardly a lover of poetry and certainly did not treat it with a poet's tenderness and belief, yet he could not but be vaguely moved by those nearby, familiar waters. Days before he had left to deliver himself up to the revolutionary adventure; he had been on the brink of death and catastrophe, and had returned there beaten and fleeing, an illegal fighter for a selfless ideal.

As night fell, they reached the doctor's village. They made for a farmhouse, where a peasant at work on the threshing floor, was surprised by the spectre of that strange group of beaten, dirty and starving men.

'But is it Doctor Ramón?'

'It is, Arturo my friend. And I need your protection.'

'Let's go to my house Doctor Ramón. We can talk better there.'

'Don't call anyone. I want us to speak alone.'

They went inside the house, through the stable and up to the floor above which smelled of hay and apples.

'First, bring us something to eat. We're all in.'

'Right away, Doctor Ramón.'

The farmhand went out and minutes later came back with an enormous loaf, a ham, and a jug of wine.

The fugitives greedily attacked the food. Even though it was essential to prepare for the escape, their hunger was such that they did not even have time to utter a single word. The farmhand was surprised by their voracious appetites and watched them curiously. Finally, the doctor said to the peasant,

'Look Arturo. You'll already have guessed that I've taken part in the revolution.'

'Yes, that's what I guessed.'

'It's finished, and they've beaten us. I need to escape to Portugal, but through Galicia where I've got friends. I thought that you would be able to help me'

'I'll do whatever you want Doctor Ramón. I'm ready to help friends when the need arises. Just tell me what has to be done.'

They talked for a long time putting together a plan. They would look for four good horses, and leave at night for Fonsagrada, guided by Arturo and another farmhand. On reaching Galicia, each would go his own way to avoid suspicion and try to enter Portugal.

'Go and make the arrangements, but don't say anything to anyone except the people I tell you to. I'm sure that everyone will help us.'

In fact, before ten o'clock that night, the pack horses were ready. Arturo put food into all the saddlebags, and the tiny caravan set off in the moonlight with the two men walking ahead. One of the fugitives who had never ridden before had to be shown how to handle his horse. The doctor who was used to riding was at the front.

They traveled like that for hours until dawn. The following day was a feast day in Fonsagrada; consequently, they came across villagers riding towards the Galician hamlet. When they were near the hamlet, the farmhands following the doctor's instructions, collected the horses and took their leave of the fugitives. The fugitives embraced and each one went his own way. The doctor walked towards the hamlet where he stayed at an inn, and that afternoon took a bus to Lugo. No one recognized him. With the help of a friend, he got into Portugal through Tuy and much later, left for France.

But other revolutionaries who had also fled into the mountains were not so fortunate. The *Guardia Civil* unceasingly hunted them down. Some fell fighting and others were captured. Broken, hungry, helpless, they gave in without glory or heroism. From then on, the waters of the two, slow running, dirty mining rivers, the Nalón and the Caudal, carried the blood of the pariahs, mixed with slag and coal from the mines.

End

Works Cited.

Alvarez, Junco J. The Emergence of Mass Politics in Spain: Populist Demagoguery and Republican Culture, 1890-1910. Portland, Ore: Sussex Academic Press, 2002. Print.

Benavides, Manuel D. *La Revolucion Fue Asi: (octubre Rojo Y Negro): Reportaje*. Barcelona, 1935.

Bunk, Brian D. "'Your Comrades Will Not Forget': Revolutionary Memory and the Breakdown of the Spanish Second Republic, 1934-1936." *History and Memory* (2002) 14:1-2: 65-92.

Casanova, Julian. *The Spanish Republic and Civil War*. Cambridge: Cambridge University Press, 2010.

Gramsci, Antonio. "Los intelectuales en España." *Cultura y Literatura*. Barcelona: Península, 1972.

Kennedy, Paul. The Spanish Socialist Party and the Modernisation of Spain. Oxford: Manchester University Press, 2015.

Lassalle, Ferdinand de. "On the Essence of Constitutions." *Marxist, www.marxists.org/history/etol/news pape/fi/vol03/no01/lassalle.htm*. Accessed 2 June 2017.

Lopez, de O. *Campana Militar De Asturias En Octubre De 1934: Narracion Tactico-Episodica*. Madrid: Yunque, 1936.

Madariaga, Salvador de. 1989. *Espana: ensayo de historia contemporanea*. Madrid: Espasa-Calpe. Print.

Peirats, Jose. *Los Anarquistas En La Guerra Civil Espanola*. Madrid: Jucar, 1977. Print.

Preston, Paul. *The Coming of the Spanish Civil War: Reform, Reaction, and Revolution in the Second Republic*. London: Routledge, 1994.

Preston, Paul. "The Origins of the Socialist Schism in Spain, 1917-31" *Journal of Contemporary History*. 12:1 (Jan., 1977): 101-132.

Rial, James H. *Revolution from Above: The Primo De Rivera Dictatorship in Spain, 1923-1930*. Fairfax: George Mason University Press, 1986.

Sender, Ramon J. *Viaje a La Aldea Del Crimen: (documental De Casas Viejas)*. Madrid: Impr. de J. Pueyo, 1934.

Shubert, Adrian. The Road to Revolution in Spain: The Coal Miners of Asturias, 1860-1934. Urbana: University of Illinois Press, 1987.

_____________. "Revolution in Self defence: the Radicalization of the Asturian Coal Miners, 1921–34." *Social History*. 7.3 (2008): 265-282.

Townson, Nigel. *La Republica Que No Pudo Ser: La Politica De Centro En Espana : 1931-1936*. Madrid: Taurus, 2002.

www.ingramcontent.com/pod-product-compliance
Lightning Source LLC
LaVergne TN
LVHW090953080826
845145LV00003B/992

* 9 7 8 1 9 4 9 9 3 8 0 9 8 *